Weblike Tales of Cold

— RK Bates —

Copyright © 2024 RK Bates
All rights reserved
First Edition

Fulton Books
Meadville, PA

Published by Fulton Books 2024

ISBN 979-8-88731-736-6 (paperback)
ISBN 979-8-88731-737-3 (digital)

Printed in the United States of America

1

Tale Driven

My mother, Beverly Miller, sat me down when I turned of age and told me the toll that taking another's life takes on the soul. "The nightmares never stop, Giovanna," she said after she told me of the tragic tale that brought about her committing this sin—a tale of love, loss, sacrifice, and human trafficking. While it's debatable whose tragic tale it was, whether it was my mother's, grandfather's, or grandmother's, this tragic tale started with young Alfonzo Ramos.

Alfonzo was only five years old when ICE came and detained his parents, eventually deporting them back to the Dominican Republic. Alfonzo was left in the care of an aunt who was rarely around and a closeted uncle-in-law who sexually abused him until he turned fifteen and ran away.

In the streets, Alfonzo was recruited by a gang he'd only heard rumors of. Over the years, after many hustles and sacrifices, Alfonzo developed a calloused heart. Using this calloused heart to manipulate situations and people, Alfonso constructed a trust system, a system which included a corrupt officer, Betronio Olson, and caseworker, Lisa Jones.

Fast forward to fall of 2016. Young Alissa Miller was told by her caseworker, Lisa Jones, that the foster system could no longer help her because she'd turned eighteen. After two weeks of observing homeless Alissa struggling to live, Betronio waited for her to sleep and kidnapped her. Betronio, right-hand man of Alfonzo, brought the girl to a huge mansion where she was introduced to Alfonzo and six others.

"Welcome to Castle Alfonzo," Alfonzo said after Alissa's blindfold was removed. He had a voice so deep it sent chills down Alissa's spine. "You, like the rest of them, are no longer your own person or the person you were before that blindfold was placed over your eyes!"

Alissa looked behind the terrifying man and noticed six witnesses, most, if not all, the same age as she.

Alfonzo handed her a driver's license. "You are twenty-one now and your new identity is Carina Davis, compliments of my friend Betronio."

Alfonzo restated his eight house rules, a reminder for the six who lived there already and for Carina. "One, I have friends in the police force and other places. Should you attempt to escape or kill me, your body will be found in a ditch twenty-four hours later!

"Two, you are all my property and basically siblings. Anyone who looks at the other the wrong way will pay when I find out!

"Three, anyone who goes out and does not bring back revenue will meet my fists!

"Four, you are all sexually versatile!

"Five, I do a curfew check every morning at two fifty, and anyone I don't find here will be found in a ditch!

"Six, everyone gets a cut of whatever they make, and whoever makes more at the end of each month gets a bonus!

"Seven, safe sex always. I will provide condoms, pills, NuvaRings, and all sorts of birth and disease prevention methods you will need!

"And eight, you never bring a guest here without my knowledge!"

After the rules were laid out, still in shock, Carina was introduced to everyone by their given identities and was told their backstories. The twins, Kyrie and Kylie Emilio, ran away from their last foster home after almost beating their foster sister to death because she bullied Kyrie for being gay and Kylie for being a transsexual woman. Valerie Clark was a former Starbucks employee who ran into Alfonzo while walking home alone one late night. Quantishia

Glazes, a former student who lived with her mom and stepfather, ran away after she was raped by her stepfather and was not believed by anyone, including her own mother. Sabrina "Queen Bee" Torres, had been kidnapped while walking home alone one afternoon from her elementary school. And lastly, Alfonzo's favorite, Giovanni Salvador, had been put in Alfonzo's care when he was only three years old, after witnessing from the back seat, his unarmed father being shot by a corrupt cop.

Despite her fear and the verbal and physical abuse that came her way, Carina adapted and did her best to obey all the rules. During the first year, she diminished Sabrina's queen bee status, experienced the loss of a household member (Kylie Emilio), and engaged in a revenue competition with the house's undefeated champion, Giovanni. She later learned the reason he was undefeated was because of his secret relationship with Juliana Thomas, a girl who resembled Carina in features, with a rich father whose only passions were hunting and giving his baby girl money.

In year two, Giovanni was approached by the god of desire in his dreams. Cupid told him the gods had decided to change whom his heart was destined to belong to—from Juliana Thomas to Carina Davis. As for Carina Davis, what made her heart ache for Giovanni was how much he cared for Kyrie Emilio, Alfonzo's least favorite and the house's least valued minority. Remembering house rule number two, Carina and Giovanni rejected each other's love until the desire to be together became too overwhelming. Finally, the two agreed to love each other immensely but in secret.

September 2018

Sabrina was someone who settled scores. She had learned of the secret relationship between Giovanni and Carina and did not hesitate to expose them. Feeling furious and betrayed by the person he considered the son he never had, Alfonzo, with Betronio's assistance, forced Giovanni to watch as he repeatedly slapped Carina across her face and then forced himself on her. In the heat of the moment, however, everyone in the house forgot house rule number seven. Days after the punishment, Carina learned she had been impregnated by a man she knew would kill her if he learned of it. And for the remainder of that month, she cried and came inches away from having an abortion. And then, as if Eileithyia, the goddess of childbirth, had a part to play, Giovanni learned of Carina's dilemma.

October 2018

After ruling out abortion, the two contemplated ways to save the unborn child, but each one ended with Alfonzo retaliating. After shopping for Halloween costumes and after a visit from Loki, the Norse god of mischief, Giovanni had a dream in which it became clear to him there was only one way out of the dilemma he and his forbidden lover found themselves in.

During Halloween night, Giovanni, who suggested Carina be DC's White Tiger, drove her to the nearest Tri-Rail. "Do you trust me?" he asked before he handed her a backpack. She nodded, confused, and took the backpack.

"I love you too much to watch anything happen to you or your unborn child. Please trust in me. If I don't come back here by 5:00 a.m., then get on a train, and go as far away from here as you possibly can and never look back." In tears, he hugged her and then drove away.

Back at Castle Alfonzo, at 1:00 a.m., "Wonder Woman" Sabrina, "Nicki Minaj" Quantishia, "Poison Ivy" Valerie, and "Betty Boop" Kyrie all prayed and crossed their fingers for "White Tiger" Carina and "Prince Charming" Giovanni to make it home before curfew.

At 1:15 a.m., Prince Charming Giovanni walked in with a White Tiger, but instead of it being Carina, it was Juliana Thomas. Though the others saw it was not Carina under the White Tiger costume after Juliana removed her head coverage, Giovanni's goal was to get her past the surveillance cameras, which everyone knew Betronio watched like a hawk. After convincing everyone Carina would beat curfew and Julian would be "Ubered" home before curfew, Giovanni persuaded the gang to engage in a game of power hour, and they agreed. Giovanni gave himself the task of walking to the fridge when someone finished, opening everyone's beverage of choice, and bringing them back new bottles. Giovanni made sure every single individual drank more than one bottle.

At 2:30 a.m., with his favorite pistol tucked in, Alfonzo rushed out of his hotel room, forgetting his cellular device on the bed. As Alfonzo drove fast to Castle Alfonzo for the curfew check, his phone received three missed calls from Betronio. Alfonzo, unaware that his destination was up in flames, stepped out of the car. Right after he closed the door of the 2018 blue Ferrari F60, a bullet carved a path to his ilium and brought him to his knees. Finally noticing his castle burning in the background, Alfonzo met eyes with the man responsible.

"What happens when all your puppets get burned?" Giovanni asked with a sinister look in his eyes and then aimed the hunting rifle he'd stolen from Juliana's father a few days before at Alfonzo's forehead.

As his heart skyrocketed, Alfonzo awaited his death.

Then something else happened. Giovanni was suddenly hit by flashbacks of nights he'd awakened screaming for his deceased father, only to be held by Alfonzo until he fell back asleep. He dropped the rifle and broke down crying. "I can't. I—" and before he had the chance to finish the thought, a bullet hit him from the back of his head.

"I saw all of them go into the living room in their Halloween costumes. I saw him bring alcohol in there, adding some type of pill in the drinks, and then he stepped outside after half an hour and began to pour gasoline all over. I tried to call you, but you were not picking up," Betronio said after Giovanni landed on the grass.

"I'm done!" Alfonzo shouted. He reached for a pistol he remembered he had on him, aimed for Betronio's neck, and pulled the trigger.

Twenty-four years later, Beverly Miller—who had been three weeks pregnant with me and lived with her mother, Alissa Miller—a woman with a deep love for tales, was working at a senior home facility, tasked primarily with caring for new arrivals. Beverly came to realize that one of the new seniors was Alfonzo Ramos. After he told her the tale of how he ended up in a wheelchair, the tale gave root to an evil bigger than mankind—revenge.

One night, as elderly Alfonzo Ramos slept, Beverly Miller sneaked in with a pillow and ended the tragic story that had been her mother's life.

2

Hidden Tales of Nemo the Fish

After our honeymoon, after unpacking, I walked downstairs and found Shane Flyer fighting the oven again. "Cooking is a nightmare," he said.

The doorbell rang.

"I got it," I told Shane. It was Amanda with Donatella. Before leaving, Shane and I had discussed the best babysitting options for Donatella and agreed on Donatella's aunty, Amanda Falcon.

"She behaved?"

"Absolutely!" Amanda said.

I doubted it but said, "Great!" anyway.

Donatella hugged me and ran up the stairs.

"Shane's cooking," I told Amanda. "Join us!" I wanted to be courteous, but deep down, I prayed for her to turn me down, remembering how sick Amanda was the last time she ate Shane's food.

"I can't. Not hungry," Amanda replied. She rushed to her car and drove away faster than I had ever seen.

He's not that bad, I thought and laughed as I closed the door.

"I'm not eating that!"

"Oh yes, you are!" I heard Shane tell Donatella before I walked back into the kitchen. She ran, and he chased her around the dining table.

When did she run back downstairs? That girl is the Flash, I thought. For almost two minutes, I watched closely as Shane failed to catch her, and then I sneaked past them, picked up the restaurant guidebook we kept on top of the refrigerator, searched for restaurants that delivered, and then I ordered.

Later, Donatella ate her dinner so fast it made me wonder if Amanda has to cook consistently when Donatella stays over.

"Will you read me the Nemo story before bed tonight, Daddy?" Donatella asked. She didn't look directly at either of us, but we both knew she meant me. The many nights I told Donatella the Nemo story, Shane stood outside the door and listened. Shane came to know the whole story, too, but Donatella never allowed Shane to tell it. I stood outside Donatella's door one night and waited for Shane to talk her to sleep. When Shane asked to tell her the Nemo story, she rejected him.

"Why can't I tell it?" Shane had asked her, offended.

"Daddy Rey tells it better," she told him.

When Shane first heard me tell Donatella the story. He waited until I lay next to him in bed and asked me, "What's the origin of that Nemo story?"

I wanted to save him the details, and so I responded, "I knew someone twenty years ago who had a four-year-old nephew who refused to sleep at night without his deceased father. She often told him that Nemo story to keep his hope alive and make him sleep."

I felt my heart break all over again—the way it had when I first found out Bianca Von Claire had overdosed. I wondered whatever happened to poor Charlie Von Claire afterward. In less than a year, the poor four-year-old, who had been abandoned by his mom at two, lost his father and aunty to drugs.

After dinner, Shane voluntarily cleaned up everything alone. As Shane scrubbed the dirty plates downstairs, I prepared Donatella for a shower. With the water running, I waited for Donatella. She came with her favorite pink towel, a gift from her mom, Cahya Falcon, for her fourth birthday. Donatella stepped in and closed the curtain and threw the towel over. I picked it up and laid it on the countertop sink.

"I'll go prepare your bed," I said and walked out of the bathroom.

* * * * *

Two days after Bianca and I learned we lived in the same neighborhood, we met at the neighborhood Target. "I will show you a secret only my brother knew," Bianca said after we decided to explore the neighborhood some more.

"*Knows*," I corrected.

Bianca gave me a confused stare.

"You said 'knew' as if your brother is no longer alive."

"He was a drug addict," she began. "We were in the same crack house."

I said no more. That's when I learned Bianca was in rehab.

When Bianca and I finally arrived at the destination, she broke the silence that the conversation about her deceased brother had created. "My brother showed me this garden after I moved into the crack house. It was our secret," she said.

I examined the garden. The grass looked lively, but it was obvious it hadn't been trimmed in ages. Ten different types of gorgeous flowers grew on top of each other. "I have not seen nature this beautiful in a long time," I told her. I looked up to follow a family of ducks that seemed unbothered by our company. "Where are they going?" I asked.

Bianca kept silent, but after the ducks arrived at their destination, I had my answer. "Most beautiful pond in the world," Bianca said. The pond was beyond magical.

I asked her about the fruits of the garden. Bianca explained, "Before that abandoned corner store was pushed out, the owners planted all sorts of stuff here. My brother told me this."

She walked closer to where I stood near some berries and picked some. I picked some also and tried to feed her, but she stopped me.

"Use your mouth instead," she demanded.

I obeyed her command, and ten seconds later, we were on the grass, caressing. The intensified moment reminded me of when I first met her.

"That was hot," Bianca said after we finished and tried to go for round two. But after joining our lips again, her phone rang.

"All right," she said to the caller.

It made me curious. *Is that her rehab house checking her whereabouts?* I wondered.

"Tell Charlie, Aunty is coming," she said, and she hung up the phone. "Come with me," she demanded. "It's ten minutes away from here."

Without question, I followed.

Ten minutes later, at a stranger's house, an older woman greeted Bianca and me. She led us to a room. "There he is," she told Bianca and vanished. I looked inside; the room was practically empty. There was a chair, a bed, a small drawer, and kid toys. "Rey, meet my nephew, Charlie. Won't sleep until he hears his favorite bedtime story." Bianca walked over and sat down on the bed. After a wave to Charlie who did not resemble Bianca, I walked over to the chair and sat down to listen.

"One day, Nemo saw another family of clownfish swimming and wondered why he and his dad were the only ones in their family. Nemo went home and asked, 'Dad how come I'm the only clownfish without a mother and brothers and sisters?' and Nemo's dad replied, 'Because the gods came to your mother in a dream and told her they needed her in heaven, a beautiful world that is full of life beyond imagining. She is preparing a home for when we join her and your brothers there. None of those members in that other family has been chosen for that yet. Consider our family lucky.' And still unimpressed, Nemo followed up with the question, 'How could Mom be in heaven? Isn't that beautiful world made only for humans?' To that, Nemo's dad said, 'A beautiful human world that needs a beautiful sea like every other, and that sea needs fish to live in it.' And Nemo asked no more questions," Bianca finished. The loud snores of Charlie took up the room. When we walked home, Bianca told me, "I think he loves that story so much because it gives him some hope that one day he and his father will be reunited."

"And his mother?" I asked.

"She disappeared when he turned two."

* * * * *

I kissed her forehead. "Good night, my princess," I told Donatella and stood up to leave. I turned around, and my eyes met Shane's. Like every other night, he stood at the doorway silently and listened. I moved closer to him; Donatella stopped me.

"Daddy Rey," she said, and her voice sounded tired, "like Nemo and his dad, when we get to heaven and find Mom and brother waiting for us, will heaven let you keep both Shane and Mommy, or will you leave Shane for Mommy?" The question stung worse than the time I was bitten by a scorpion. What made it worse was the fact that I knew they were both waiting on an answer, and neither one would sleep without one. No, what made it worse was knowing the answer I had in mind was going to hurt one of them, even if that hurt was not intentional.

"Well, my princess," I began and turned to face her instead of Shane, "if heaven wants me to just have one of them and that's what your heart desires, then, yes, I'd leave Shane for your mother without blinking."

I looked back, and Shane was gone.

After I turned off the lights and closed the door, I walked into our room and found Shane already in bed and his back turned to me. I said nothing, lay down next to him, and slept.

3

Beautiful Syndrome Tale

It happened during her two-year vacation away from music. She sang, and the crowd went crazy. They loved it! Everyone was enjoying the moment, that is, all except one person. This troubled her enough to make her walk over as soon as the performance ended, without signing any autographs. She ordered one of her bodyguards to ask the young lady who sat next to him to give up her barstool.

"You know, everyone is going wild for me, but you're not. Kind of like how everyone nearly passed out when I walked in, and you didn't."

He did not reply. Instead, he waited for her to ask him a question.

"What is it? Haven't you heard of me?"

Finally, there it was, the question he'd waited for from the moment he watched her step off the stage and walk over. "I know who you are. I don't go crazy over fraud celebrities. As great as your songs may be, you only live for what the crowd wants."

Though she felt insulted, she knew he told her the truth, and she admired that about him. "Well, I am spending eleven months away from the music industry. I could use a fine gentleman to show me around. It would be an opportunity to show me how to not be a fraud when I return." She caught the bartender's attention, and then she covered his tab.

He knew he would regret agreeing to the idea, but he was too prideful not to accept such an invitation. "I am Bohen Jones," he told her, and then she introduced herself too.

After they exchanged contact information, Bohen and the celebrity grabbed coffee the following day. "Make mine a regular black coffee," he told the waitress.

"Make mine a grande," she said. The three of them laughed.

"Clever," he told her, "I see that you are a dangerous woman indeed!"

What should have been just an eleven-month fling became more. Bohen and the celebrity enjoyed each other's company too much. Bohen gave his heart to her. Nine months later, Bohen and the celebrity welcomed a baby girl. However, she was not what either of them imagined their first child would be like.

"What's wrong with her?" the celebrity asked after the doctor handed her the beautiful redhead baby.

"Nothing at all," Bohen replied before the doctor said what they were thinking. And when the eleventh month finally arrived, Bohen remembered the first night he met the celebrity and how he knew he would have eventually regretted the decision he made that night.

"I can't go back to the industry with this baby. It would kill my music career, and we both know it!" she argued before she handed him a check she had written the day before. "I'll make sure you and she are taken care of. A new check every month for confidentiality."

As Bohen felt his heart break into a million pieces, he made a vow to never love anyone again, except his daughter. "Confidentiality? Keep your money and disappear. Arian and I will do fine without it!" That was the last time Bohen saw the celebrity either in real life or on television.

Fast-forward, four years. Bohen and Arian stepped out of the house and began to walk on the sand. *I forgot what this felt like*, Bohen thought and remembered evacuating to his sister's house after the news announced that hurricane Irma had increased a category.

"Any time you guys need a runaway from your beach condo, feel free to come to my house," Bohen remembered his sister, Lisa Jones, saying. Bohen knew his sister all too well, and he knew she meant it.

On their way back, after three miles, Bohen spotted something. It was almost completely covered by sand, but the little part that was not shined in the sunlight. He let go of Arain's hand and bent down to see what it could be. Bohen picked up the string attached to the shiny object, and it revealed a beautiful shell—one crafted in the shape of a seahorse. "I've never seen such beauty," Bohen said before washing off the sand and then placing the necklace around Arian's tiny neck. "Don't let anyone take it from you!" he told her, and she nodded.

Nighttime came. Arian, whom Bohen had constantly told to not sneak out and go to the beach at night, silently pushed the backyard door open and disobeyed. "We will find you one, too, Barbie," Arian told her doll before she heard a voice talking from a distance. Curious, Arian walked until the voice was close enough. "It's coming from behind that rock, Barbie," she announced to the doll before she looked.

"Whoa...you're a mermaid!" Arian said and immediately thought of her *Little Mermaid* doll back at home.

The mermaid, who seemed frustrated, and who had never seen such a small human in person, was also amazed. "Yes, my name is Mia, and I am searching for a magical necklace my father gave me when I was a little girl. My pet seahorse ran away, and I went after her. There was a storm, and then I lost it!"

Arian knew exactly what the mermaid was looking for. "Here!" Arian said and took off the necklace. "Daddy and I found it this morning," she added after the mermaid took it from her hand with a graceful smile.

"Thank you so much for being so kind and honest. You must have a lot of small human friends."

"No. The kids in my class always make fun of me. Daddy said it's because I was born with a gift called syndrome." And before the mermaid had a chance to comment, Arian went on, "I don't get it. If it's a gift, then why do they hate me?"

"Because they wanted to be born with that gift. They're jealous," the mermaid replied, pulling Arian's chin up with one finger. She turned Arian around and placed the necklace back on her neck. "You should keep it. My name is Princess Mia of Belleza, and I want to be your friend."

That marked the beginning of their friendship. At nighttime, the two met at the same spot and discussed their day, drank tea on the beach with Barbie, and listened to each other sing.

After dinner, one night, after Arian watched Lisa drive away, she confessed it to her dad. "Dad, I made a new friend named Mia. She's a mermaid, and I want you to meet her!"

Bohen, seeing the excitement in his daughter's face, almost gave life to his heart again. "That's exciting, my princess. I am very happy for you, but before I meet Mia, you should describe her to me." He watched the smile on her face enlarge as she began.

"Well, Mia has long and curly and red hair. She has pink lips and dark-blue eyes just like Barbie. She's very magical. She can change her mermaid tail into legs by just thinking about it!"

"Oh my god! I can't wait to meet her!" Bohen said excitedly and picked up his daughter, hugged her, and then spun her across the room. The next night, the introduction was made, and it was everything she described.

At bedtime, Arian begged her father to let Mia come into her room at night to have tea inside, and her father approved. "Can Mia be my new babysitter too? I don't like Juliana Thomas."

Bohen did not approve that idea, but he worked with her. "Juliana can watch television in the living room while you and Mia and Barbie play in your room." That idea made her happy. After reading her a bedtime story, he turned on the nightlight, kissed her on the cheek, wished her good night, and walked out.

The next morning, as Bohen and Arian were about to finish their daily three-mile walk, Bohen saw it—blood running down his beautiful daughter's nose right before she collapsed in his arms. With

Mia by his side, Bohen rushed through traffic, passed through security, and handed his daughter to the first doctor he laid eyes on.

"Mia, am I going to die like my mommy?" Arian asked when she opened her eyes and saw Mia standing there with flowers she'd collected near the beach.

"No, baby. That necklace has magic, and it will heal you," Mia told her.

Bohen walked in. "My little warrior is finally up," he said with a smile at Mia. He handed Arian her Barbie, hugged her on the bed, and then told her, "Daddy loves you so much!"

Three people followed him into the room. "Mr. Jones," one of them said to get his attention. He turned around and saw the doctor who had operated on his beautiful daughter, with a young male and female nurse. They all had serious looks on their faces. "Let's talk outside!" the doctor said, and Bohen followed them out.

He walked back into the room after a half hour and gave his daughter a smile. "You're going to be fine," he told her, and it made her smile. "But after the doctor told me that, I received a call from a job I applied for in New York. I have to leave in two days, but when the doctor releases you a week from now, I want you to stay with Mia at her house until I come for you." He expected her to be saddened by this, but she was not. She was more than excited to finally explore Mia's world.

"Okay, Daddy!" she said happily. When he looked at how happy he'd made her, he felt his heart finally opened again.

Two weeks later, as her daddy promised, Mia came to the hospital and told Arian it was time. Mia drove Arian back to the beach. "Close your eyes. Sing and think of mermaid tails," Mia told her.

Arian, who craved this new adventure more than anything she had ever craved in her four years of life, obeyed without question. Mia and Arian jumped in the water. Mia led the way.

As Mia had described to her, during one of their teas, Belleza was the most magical place Arian had ever seen. The fish told her great stories; the dolphins sang all her favorite songs; and the seahorses played with her. Mia even told her to keep one of them. Her name was Amelica. Mia then introduced Arian to her royal family. Mia's father, the king of Belleza, promoted Arian to be Mia's primary trusted advisor. Mia's mother, the queen, had six gardens and gave Arian one. Mia's brother, the prince, announced he'd only consider Arian for queen if he was to be king.

Twenty-one years passed. The magic of Belleza caused Arian to forget about her father's promise to come back for her. And during her twenty-sixth birthday, after she kissed the prince during their wedding ceremony, Arian kneeled and waited to be crowned queen of Belleza. After the crown was placed, Arian stood back up, and that's when her eyes met his. It was Bohen who crowned her.

"It took longer than I thought, but I am here now, my queen," Bohen said and opened his arms for her to jump in like old times.

4

Tales of Tri-Rail F

Cassandra Ortiz stepped out of the taxi with her one carry-on and gave the taxi driver a confused look. "Head east for ten minutes. You can't miss it," he told her before he made a U-turn and drove away. As she walked away, Cassandra remembered everything Jacob Karbono, her ex-boyfriend who disappeared without a trace, used to tell her about the infamous Tri-Rail F. He never told her what the F stood for, but he did tell her about how Tri-Rail F was rumored to have existed before Christ and was operated in the shadows until someone exposed its existence to the world in the year 2013.

"He stumbled upon it accidentally. Bad for them. He was a journalist with an intense hunger for recognition," Jacob explained, when Cassandra wondered how the exposure came about. Jacob told her that Tri-Rail F worked to free people they felt were in need of saving from earth or themselves. "I hear the four trains, often packed with passengers, travel to four magical worlds that are not even on the map!"

Hearing these fantastic things made Cassandra wonder. "How can someone buy tickets? Where would they need to go?" Cassandra badly desired the answer, primarily because she knew how vital it was for her to get away from her cruel life.

"We don't decide who's going, only the owner of the station does. Everyone calls him the Operator. He's a mystery to us all."

"How does the Operator decide?" Cassandra asked.

Jacob explained, "Well, I hear he has people who work in the shadows. Rumor has it, they spy on all of us. If they choose one of us for one of their four special trains, then the person receives a call from the Operator."

When Cassandra finally arrived, she remembered what the taxi driver said. *This has to be the place*, Cassandra thought as she looked at the tall medieval fortified tower. She remembered Jacob telling her that Tri-Rail F was remodeled, and seeing it in person made her wonder how long ago they remodeled. Creating a barrier around the tower, which had only one entrance and no window openings, was a wall constructed entirely out of marble so long and tall that it shamed the Great Wall of China. When Cassandra walked in, she finally noticed the remodeling. The inside had a reception desk, and like its surroundings, it was modern. Cassandra saw a line, and she waited her turn. When she finally reached the guy who sat at the reception desk, he handed her a printed ticket and then told her, "Keep it to yourself. Go out through the door behind me, and wait for your train to come."

Cassandra obeyed. She located the door he mentioned and walked out of it as he ordered, to a plain, grassy field with four nearby train tracks and some benches. *It almost looks like a normal train station*, Cassandra thought before a lady with a small handbag began to walk toward her.

"So ready for this mysterious adventure that no one ever returns from?" the lady asked.

Cassandra gave her a smile and prayed for her to go start a conversation with someone else.

"The Operator has got to be the greatest human being alive. A few days after our honeymoon, my husband and I found out about my metastatic breast cancer. I looked at my husband and our three-year-old daughter and cried because I thought that was the end of my story, of our story. And then, two nights after, I received a call from the Operator. Rumor has it, there are doctors where I am going who can tackle even stage four cancers."

Even though she did not want to, Cassandra felt her heart desiring to pity the lady.

"I'm Maya," the lady said, and Cassandra shook her hand, tossing aside the desire she had to tell the lady to go bother someone else. She looked around, and there were at least two hundred people in the empty field. Maya asked Cassandra what was the last thing that happened to her before she received her call from the Operator.

"Well, growing up down here was always awful for me. Ever since I was just five, all I knew was heartache, misery. As you can see, I am not slim. The kids made fun of me every day and gave me the nickname Fat Hippo-Sandra."

Cassandra, without any warning, broke down in tears, until Maya hugged her and calmed her down.

"One day when I couldn't take all the bullying anymore, I took a chair and a rope and tried to take my own life. Luckily for me, Dad came home early from work that afternoon. He made it in time to save me, but the next morning, I received a call from the Operator."

"What about your mother?" the lady asked, and Cassandra told her how her mother had disappeared from their lives and never returned. As silence fell between them, Cassandra admired the four train tracks, and they made her wonder.

"If the worlds each train goes to are all beautiful and set people free, why must there be a choice?"

"The same reason we have ten thousand different candies and cable companies."

"The Operator said not to give anyone my ticket. Has anyone ever switched tickets?" Maya shook her head, as curious and confused as Cassandra.

"I don't think it's ever been done. Can I see your train number?" Maya asked. Cassandra remembered the Operator's words and almost hesitated. But she did not. Cassandra did not know why she felt that way, but something inside her convinced her to trust this stranger more than she ever trusted anyone in her entire life.

Cassandra showed Maya her train number and waited for a reaction, but Maya did not provide any direct one.

"Train number two is nice, I heard," Maya said, and then Cassandra heard the rumbling sound of the approaching trains.

"Quick goodbye hug. I have train number one," Maya said, and before Cassandra had a chance to agree or disagree, she pulled her in tightly and held on for a full minute.

"Enjoy it all," Maya said and walked closer to the train tracks.

The trains arrived, and to Cassandra's surprise, they were not constructed with any entrance or exit doors. Instead, the trains had a bunch of tentacle-like tubes that descended from the top and pulled people inside, by their ticket numbers. Train number two, which had more tentacles than the other three, for reasons Cassandra was curious about, pulled Maya inside. Cassandra felt confused, but not as confused as she felt when the tentacle that pulled her came from train number one instead of two.

After train number one disappeared and then reappeared over a new ocean, as Jacob had described, Cassandra experienced the magic that she had only heard rumors of. "I hear even the animals can talk. And that nothing gets sick there!" Cassandra remembered Jacob saying after she looked outside the windows and witnessed it herself. First, Cassandra watched, as families of clownfish sang a welcoming song for the passengers and then as a beautiful young girl with a mermaid tail, riding on the back of a dolphin with two followers behind her, a glowing seahorse necklace on her neck, and a crown on the head, showed the passengers the neat tricks that she and her dolphin were capable of.

When train number one finally landed, like magic, the tentacles vanished and doors appeared. "Whoaaa!" Cassandra said when she stepped out of the train and laid eyes on the beautiful, natural island that awaited her. *Wait*, Cassandra thought, *why did Maya switch our tickets and give up all of this?* Then her eyes landed on someone.

He ran to her and picked her up before she could process what she was seeing. He swung her around in excitement. "Oh my god, I am so happy you came!" Jacob told her excitedly, and this made her smile. The smile, however, did not last long.

"Jacob, how'd you? Why didn't you t—"

"I was coming from soccer practice one night and saw this one guy stalking that chick Valerie who worked at Starbucks. He had a gun, but I was bold. I grabbed his gun and fought him off. After Valerie and I called the police and told them what happened, I went home. When I arrived home, I received a call from the Operator. When someone gets the call, they can't even tell family. That's why I did not tell you." Jacob touched Cassandra's soft skin and then kissed her the way he used to.

As the magic happened around her, as she enjoyed Jacob's strawberry-flavored lips, Cassandra wondered, *Where do those three other trains go?*

* * * * *

Back home, Jesse Ortiz sat patiently in the support circle and waited for his turn to talk. "His name was Giovanni, and he was my only family, my only son. Ever since his death, I have felt as though nothing in life matters anymore," Alfonzo Ramos said. He was the closest friend Jesse had in the support group. Jesse always wondered how he ended up in a wheelchair but never asked out of respect.

Jesse's turn came right after his friend, Alfonzo, finished; and he told the crowd, "When my little Cassandra was three, I lost my beautiful wife, Maya, to breast cancer, and so I told Cassandra her mother just walked out on us, to spare her the pain. Recently, Cassandra hung hers...," and Jesse broke down, crying. Alfonzo opened his arms, the way he did for his deceased son whenever something was wrong and welcomed Jesse in.

5

Mirrorman Tale

Betronio Olson was only sixteen years old when he first met Mirrorman. It was by accident of course. "Don't you eat enough blobfish?" his stepdad said, one evening, at the dinner table. Of course, his mom was not around. Though if she was, he's sure she would not have done much about it. Betronio remembered the afternoon he came crying home to his mom about the name his bullies at school had come up with for him. Though his mom did nothing to help him, his stepdad kept the name and used it regularly ever since that day.

"Leave me the fuck alone!"

"I just got hungry!" Betronio yelled in an effort to end the name-calling. He tried this so many times before.

"Your fat ass is always hungry!" And before Betronio could take a piece of that delicious bread that his mother always made, his stepdad pulled it away from his hand and tossed it on the floor. "No profanity in this house, fat ass!" he yelled at Betronio before smacking him across the face.

"Go to your room, blobfish!" his stepdad ordered, and with tears running down his face, Betronio simply obeyed.

"I can't do this anymore!" Betronio cried, with a small butter knife he stole from the dinner table aimed at his own throat. Betronio, who did not expect a response because he thought he was completely alone in the room, then heard a voice. It came from his closet.

"Right here, smart-ass." Betronio heard as he searched the closet. It came from the mirror that once hung at the top of his bed. Betronio looked in the mirror and saw him. It was him, but at the same time it was not. The reflection, the one with the voice of its own, looked exactly like Betronio, except it was bald and anorexic.

"Who are you?" Betronio asked, almost terrified at what he was experiencing. To Betronio, the scene was almost as scary as his walk home from after-school tutoring. Betronio was convinced there was always someone hiding in the shadows, stalking him, waiting to make a move.

"Isn't it obvious?" asked the figure in the mirror.

"I'm the less fatty version of you of course. I was sent to save you from all this pain." After he said this, Betronio felt a loss of control over his own body. All Betronio knew was that he could still control what he wanted to say, nothing more or less. "Let's get to work!" the man in the mirror said, and Betronio's foot began to move on its own. Out of the room, all the way back to the dinner table, where his stepdad finished the rest of that delicious bread.

"You can tell the world Mirrorman has arrived, bitch!" Betronio whispered into his stepdad's ears before slitting his throat. Betronio's mom came home and asked him about his stepdad, and Betronio told her he had no idea. The body was never discovered; all his belongings were gone; and so she assumed he just took off, like the guys she was with before.

In school, Betronio's three main bullies were the triplets Johnny, John, and Jonas Dynasty. One day, while sitting at lunch and contemplating if he should tell Mirrorman about the triplets, Britney Sanders, the new girl and rumored to be the hottest girl in school, sat down next to Betronio. "I'm Britney," she said, and he looked around to make sure she was talking to him.

Why is such a hot girl talking to a fat, loser like me? Betronio wondered.

"Me?" he asked, just to confirm she was talking to him. And after she nodded, Betronio discreetly pinched himself.

"I think you're adorable. We should be study buddies. Maybe more," she said with a wink. Betronio felt his heart grow wings and flew away. He was never this happy. No one, except his mom, has ever been nice to him before.

Betronio ran home after school tutoring ended, briefly greeted his mom, and then closed his door. "Mirrorman! Mirrorman! Mirrorman!" he yelled repeatedly until his slimmer look-alike finally appeared, with a smile so twisted it almost cracked the mirror he was trapped inside.

"What's the news?" Mirrorman asked, and then rephrased the question, "I meant to ask what's the tea?"

"Britney Sanders likes me. I know she wants to be my girlfriend!" Betronio said excitedly and jumped up and down, as far up as his weight allowed him to go, of course. To Betronio's surprise, Mirrorman did not seem as excited as he was.

"You poor blobfish, she's using you for something, obviously. A beautiful, model-like girl like Britney Sanders with a fat hippo such as yourself?" said the man in the mirror, with a sympathetic voice.

"No!" Betronio yelled before he picked up his *Terminator* action figure and aimed it at the center of the mirror. "You're just jealous!" Then tossed it like an upset three-year-old, leaving spiderweb-like cracks on the mirror.

Betronio was not bothered by the triplets or anyone else anymore. Everyone heard about Britney's brother being an MMA fighter, and so no one messed with Betronio. The next two school years, junior and senior years, were the best in Betronio's entire life, all thanks to all the great times he had with Britney Sanders.

However, two days before graduation, Betronio had discovered the scheme. With an attempt to surprise Britney with a pregraduation gift, Betronio walked to her house. Betronio knew exactly where Britney and her parents kept the extra set of keys for the backyard door and let himself in. He quietly walked up the stairs to her room, and right as he was about to knock, Betronio heard a familiar voice. It was Britney's best friend, Julia Thomas.

"Thank god you can finally end this pretend relationship and finally go public with Johnny," Julia said. Betronio waited for Britney's response before reacting.

"It was exhausting, but my GPA was worth it. Who knew fat people could be so needy." Britney replied, and Betronio felt those wings that his heart had grown grinded down to pieces. Betronio ran home as fast as he could, tossing the roses and Beyonce's tickets on a nearby trash can. Without greeting his mom, Betronio ran to his room and locked the door.

He searched his closet and then began to pull off the towels he used to cover the cracked mirror. *It's been two years. He's probably gone,* Betronio thought as he removed the towels. To Betronio's surprise, he was wrong. Through the cracks, Betronio saw Mirrorman. Mirrorman did not age a day, nor did he gain a single pound since Betronio saw him last.

"Let's bury a hoe tonight!" Mirrorman yelled before Betronio even said anything.

Betronio lost control of his body again and later found himself at a cemetery, with a shovel in hand. When he did not see Britney Sanders at graduation, Betronio knew Mirrorman was behind it.

The case of missing high school graduate Britney Sanders had hit the news more than once, and it bothered Betronio every single time. One day, Betronio just had enough.

"Goodbye, Mirrorman," Betronio said before covering the cracked mirror back with the towels and taking it outside to the dumpster.

"You'll regret this! You'll need me your whole life, blobfish!" Betronio heard from the dumpster, as he walked away in tears and regrets.

One late night, as Betronio walked down that same creepy street he used to walk home after school, he ran into them—the triplets. It was four months later, and Betronio assumed the triplets had already moved away for college.

"I know it was you. You killed Britney!" Johnny Dynasty said angrily before John and Jonas held Betronio tightly. "You will pay!" Johnny added and then began to practice his boxing skills on Betronio's guts. After he was tired of punching Betronio, Johnny pulled out a pistol and hit Betronio with the back, dropping Betronio on his butt. "Say hi to Brit for us!" Johnny said and aimed the pistol at Betronio's head. Before Johnny pulled the trigger, that creepy figure Betronio knew was always hidden in the shadows appeared under the lights finally.

"I don't think it's fair how there's three of you and only one of him. Let him get up, and let's make this a fair fight!" The figure said, and to Betronio's surprise, he did not look much older than the rest of them. Johnny turned his pistol and pointed at the figure's head instead, but then another shot was fired from the shadows and hit Johnny on the left eye. After Johnny's body touched the ground, the figure fired repeatedly at John and Jonas who tried to make a run for it. After John and Jonas followed Johnny to the ground, each with a bullet at the back of their heads, the figure offered Betronio his hand.

"I'm Alfonzo Ramos," and Betronio did not know why, but it felt as though he had just discovered a new mirrorman.

6

Unborn Tale

Julia Thomas sat in her office and just stared at the date on the calendar. Julia had a ton of paperwork in front of her, but her focus just would not shift. *How does one go about not thinking about an upcoming abortion date?* Julia wondered as she heard a knock on the door. "It's open!" Julia said, and he walked in.

Wisner T Flyer was Julia's top employee despite speaking the least amount of English in the restaurant. Even Julia's husband, Andrew, often asked Julia about Wisner when she got home. Andrew only had a few conversations with Wisner here and there, but he could never brag enough about how hard Wisner worked.

"Wis," Julia said and remembered she had not scheduled Wisner to work that day. "Have a seat. What are you doing here?"

"Thank you, boss," Wisner replied before sitting down on the chair farthest from Julia, sending a signal he knew she'd understand. "Nine months before, me go back to Haiti, and me wife is giving baby soon. Me gone back to Haiti two days, and me not coming back early."

Julia, having talked to Wisner more than all the other employees in the restaurant, understood everything he'd said without a drop of sweat. He had impregnated his wife when he went on vacation nine months before, Julia confirmed to herself; and now that she was almost due, he was going back and was not sure when he would be returning.

"Oh no. Wisner, you are my number one! This place won't be the same without you." At that moment, a series of flashbacks hit Julia—flashbacks of all the times she'd locked the office from inside and explored every part of Wisner's body. Some nights, he pinned her to the wall next to all her important papers. Other nights, she made him clear off her desk the best he could and penetrate through. Those nights did not end in the office. Julia relived them all in her mind on the days Wisner was off. There were nights she could not even force herself to relive because they were dirtier than any type of porn the world had to offer.

"Yes, boss lady," Wisner said. He picked up his last few checks from where Julia usually left them to be picked up and turned to leave.

"Have you and your wife decided on a name?" she asked before he opened the door.

"Well, me wife sure baby be a boy. We gonna name him Shane."

Shane Flyer, that has such a ring to it, Julia thought, and it made her a little jealous. All she wanted to do in that very moment is confess to Wisner that she was about to abort her baby soon, a baby she was one hundred percent sure he was the real father of.

"Wis," Julia said, and Wisner gave her his full attention. Before she could say it, Julia remembered her husband, Andrew, and how she would destroy him. *Andrew's too good of a guy for me to be that cruel,* she told herself, and Julia stopped.

"Thank you for everything. Goodbye." Julia gave Wisner a final hug.

When Julia finally made it home, she prepared herself a small microwavable dinner. Andrew was on a hunting trip with his friends, so she did not feel pressured to cook a proper meal. Julia did not sleep much; instead, she stared at the ceiling and felt guilty about Wisner not knowing about her pregnancy and about telling Andrew the reason she could not keep the child was because she could not afford to have a kid at that time of her life.

Julia woke up before sunrise and went back to work on her garden. After Julia dropped a seed into the ground and piled dirt over it, she noticed the tiny feet. Julia looked up and saw a little boy. He could not have been older than five.

"Hello."

Julia smiled politely, just in case his parents were nearby. "What's your name?"

"My name is Charlie, but everyone calls me Little Charlie because...," the little boy searched for the rest of his sentence.

Kids, Julia thought and rolled her eyes. "Well, where are your parents, Little Charlie? Where do you live?"

"I live in the yellow house. It's new. My mommy is away on a business trip, and I've been staying with my babysitter. She's mean. Can I help you?"

Julia was surprised that a new house had been built on the block and she'd missed it. *It must be all this abortion thinking,* she convinced herself. Julia gave Little Charlie a trowel after she took his teddy bear, who he told her was named Pooh after *Winnie-the-Pooh,* and put it where it would not get dirty. After gardening, she welcomed Little Charlie inside and made him pancakes with Nutella spread all over, with a glass of orange juice to wash it down, and then she cleaned him. Before she drove to work, she watched him head in the direction of his house.

At the same time the next morning, Little Charlie appeared at the same spot. "Come back here around five, and we'll go see a G-rated movie together," Julia said after Charlie left her house. He did show up; she saw him by the front door as she pulled into the garage. She cooked dinner for two, and they ate, and then drove to the nearest movie theater. She remembered he told her his curfew was eight o'clock, and she made sure he was home fifteen minutes before.

On the fourth day, Julia went to the fair for the very first time. It was terrifying, but Little Charlie made it less so. "It's not scary when you get used to it," he told her when they stepped off the rollercoaster.

"Miss Julia, do you love your job?" Little Charlie asked on the drive home.

The question surprised Julia. "I'm what I've wanted to be. I own my restaurant and hotel. What do you want to be when you grow up?"

"A business owner like you Miss Julia." And this made Julia smile. She knew he'd change his mind when he grew up.

On the fifth day, Little Charlie and Julia went grocery shopping together. It was Halloween, so Julia dressed as Cruella de Vil, and Little Charlie dressed as one of the dalmatians.

"Aww, you and your son are the most beautiful thing I've seen all day. You guys are adorable!" The cashier said, and everyone in the line agreed. Julia did not bother telling them he was not her son because she felt it was unnecessary.

On the tenth day, Little Charlie did not come. After she pulled into her parking lot later that day and did not find him waiting outside the front door, it made her wonder. When she walked in, however, Andrew's smelly hunting boots greeted her. *He's home*, she thought. She rushed upstairs and kissed him.

"I missed you so much," she told him over dinner, about an hour or so later.

"I missed you too. You got the thing done though?" he asked, referring to the abortion procedure he helped her schedule. She nodded and told him it was done earlier that day.

"It's what you wanted, and I support you no matter what," he said, and it made her happy.

"If we did have the child, what names would you have given it?" Julia asked.

"Well, the same names I'll use when we do decide to have kids when you're ready. If we have a girl, I think Juliana Thomas, and for a boy, Little Charlie Thomas," Andrew replied.

Julia drove by the same spot the next morning and saw there was no longer a yellow house.

"It was just there a few days ago. I swear!" she told Andrew before she broke down in tears.

7

Tales of Lie

Before Julia switched her last name from Thomas to Rosario, she had Andrew. Andrew treated Julia like a queen, but the guilt she felt after aborting what could've been their first child became too consuming. It weighed on her on a daily basis. Julia did not find the courage to tell Andrew about the affair until the first birthday of their daughter, Juliana. Julia could not explain it, but no other time felt right.

The confession, as Julia had not predicted, turned Andrew into someone unrecognizable. He went through great lengths to make sure he won the custody battle, and coming from a successful and rich family, which included two cutthroat lawyers, made it extremely easy for Andrew. How it all played out left Julia distraught. She never imagined she'd ever experience a pain as bad as the one she'd felt when her high school best friend, Britney Sanders, was announced dead a few days before their high school graduation. However, her divorce proved her wrong.

Seven months after the divorce, Julia met Mauricio Rosario during a vacation in the Dominican Republic, where she traveled to get away from the drama. Julia learned Mauricio, although a Dominican, was only visiting from America. Julia did not want to risk losing Mauricio, a guy she believed was her chance at redemption, so she proposed three months after the introductory phase. By then they had returned to America. Though he rejected her proposal, Mauricio proposed to her a week later.

When Julia finally brought up the conversation about having a family with Mauricio, he told her about his male infertility. He offered to leave her, to make her happy and keep her dream about having a family alive, but she did not allow it. Instead, Julia agreed for them to adopt a child. After their marriage, they adopted a beautiful baby boy and named him Rafael Rosario. He was only three years older than his stepsister, Juliana Thomas. Julia, despite the struggles of co-parenting with Andrew, lived a great life with Mauricio, his loving mother, and Rafael.

When little Rafael turned six, his parents went to a white-themed party and did not return.

"Grandma, why aren't Mommy and Daddy back yet?" Rafael asked.

His grandma called him over to where she sat on the sofa. Before she said anything, she covered him with the long blanket she used every night when she watched late-night movies.

"Remember all the stories I told you about the Operator?" she began.

Rafael nodded, and she continued, "Well, your parents were great people who were loved by everyone they met. They did everything right in their life, and the Operator called them tonight. I think they have been chosen for train number one."

"Without me, Grandma?" Rafael asked. Then the tearworks began.

"Don't cry. If in your own life you do exactly the things your parents did in theirs, then one day the Operator will call you, too, and you'll be put in train number one like them. The three of you will live happily forever."

Rafael relaxed after hearing this. He knew he had to do everything his parents would have done in every situation. *It's the only way we will be reunited and live forever in a beautiful and magical world,* Rafael thought.

"Grandma, I forgot to tell you, there's a boy in my class that says there are four trains and not two. One girl even said her mom told her there are really five trains," Rafael said. He began to feel sleepy.

"All of that is rubbish, my boy. There's train number one, and then there's train number two, that's it," she told him, a bit angry that people still believed there were more than two trains. After she told him this, he finally fell asleep. She waited five more minutes and then carried him to his room.

The first introduction was made in March of 2017. He must have been twenty-one at that time. Rafael was twenty-two years old, a year older than he. It happened by accident. Rafael worked as a bartender at The Office around that time, but he was off the night he saw Reyman Debroyi. He was drinking his beer, dancing in the crowded space, and minding his own business when he saw Giovanni Salvador, his half-sister's prostitute boyfriend, flirting with Reyman at the bar. Reyman seemed to Rafael to be uninterested and in need of saving, so Rafael went to the rescue.

"My boyfriend is too nice to say he's not interested," Rafael said and gave Giovanni the dirtiest look that came to mind. Giovanni knew him well. Giovanni knew he did not want Rafael to out his secret. Giovanni disappeared, and Rafael did not see him for the remainder of that night.

Rafael took the available seat and said, "Some guys just can't take a hint. He is a prostitute. The first time I met him, he tried to trick me into sleeping with him for money. Lucky for me I have a gift. I can spot a prostitute from a mile away." To Rafael's surprise, Reyman did not say anything at all the entire night. Instead, he touched Rafael's lap and gave him a look. It started with a kiss at the bar, and then the two continued at Rafael's house.

Rafael woke up in the middle of the night and found Reyman dressed to leave. "One-night stand?" Rafael asked and felt disappointed. *I really thought this one was different*, he thought.

"Sorry, handsome. Turns out your prostitute radar was off tonight. Pay up," Reyman said and tossed Rafael his wallet. With the money, Reyman disappeared.

Rafael worked at The Office more frequently, hoping to run into him again, but luck was not on his side.

In the fall of 2027, the two reunited. Rafael never saw it coming. He came home one night and collapsed in front of his girlfriend.

Aida Fazil, who was never taught how to react in emergencies, did the first thing that came to her mind—she gave in to a panic attack. Luckily one of her brothers, Akeem, was there. Akeem dialed 911, and before he blinked, they were outside. Aida and Akeem watched in terror as the ambulance drove away with Rafael. The two thought of their parents, neither of them wanted to relive the nightmare of losing someone else they loved so much.

"Doctor?" Akeem asked, as Aida just stood there, unable to speak. This was not new for Aida; Akeem was always her savior. She never admitted to it out loud, but she loved him more than her other three siblings.

"Your friend is dealing with end-stage renal disease. In order to stay alive, he'll need a kidney transplant. Any volunteers?"

While this should have been easy for Aida to do, something inside her went completely against it. She loved Rafael more than anyone she'd ever met. She trusted him more than her own siblings at times, but her gut did not agree with donating a kidney. She always listened to her guts.

"Aida, you have two. Why are you so scared to give him one?" Akeem asked her later. They sat and discussed it with their other siblings over dinner.

"Do it," Anivens, one of her brothers, suggested. However, her sister Aisha disagreed completely.

"Sister, you never know. The surgery is very risky, and I don't think it's worth the risk."

"Just pay an organ donor. They don't mind the risk," Ajmal, Aida's other brother, said. Among all of them, Aida decided Ajmal gave her the best advice, so she did that. Aida made it a priority, even contacting former friends of her mother. When she hit dead ends, she continued.

Aida was ready to give up, when, blessed by fate, she received a call from an organ donor.

"My name is Reyman Debroyi. I've never donated an organ before, but I want to do this. I met your boyfriend once, and someone with a heart like his should not have to die. If I can, I want to save his life, with the condition that you keep your money."

Without a second thought, Aida agreed to the terms. The next morning, Aida called the doctor and confirmed it was not too late for Rafael. The surgery was successful, but with that success came heartbreak. A month later, Rafael sat Aida down and told her he had fallen for another.

"A while back, I would've loved you for eternity. Ever since the surgery, I haven't felt like the Rafael you knew, and I don't think it's fair for me to keep you around when I feel my heart slowly pulling away. I will always have a place for you in my heart but as friends," he admitted.

The heartbreak tore Aida apart. If not for the comfort of her four siblings, Aida believed it would have driven her insane, but Rafael moved on.

In 2030, Rafael tried the white suit on and walked out to show Anivens. "Well?" Rafael asked, and Anivens rejected it.

"Basic," Anivens told him. Rafael trusted Anivens and whatever opinion he had because Rafael knew he was an honorable friend. Unlike Akeem, who cut all ties with Rafael after he broke things off with Aida, even though Rafael and Aida became best friends.

"The wedding is in three days, so if this one is bad, then so be it. Rey will understand," Rafael said before he walked out wearing the last outfit.

"I love it," Anivens said. It was white, like the one he'd tried on before, but something about it felt like a powerful statement to Rafael, and so he kept it.

The night before the wedding, Rafael dreamt of his grandmother. Rafael woke up on a beautiful island where magic replaced oxygen, where the impossible existed more frequently than the possible. *This has to be the magical place the Operator trains take people to*, Rafael thought as he remembered the amazing stories his grandmother used to tell him. "Rafi," he heard someone say and turned to find his grandmother standing there. She looked as if she was in her early thirties. This did not surprise Rafael.

"Grandma, you left me. What happened?" Rafael asked as tears ran down his face.

"Well, I told you the Operator was going to call me to come here with your parents. Sad to say that you have lost your ticket to join us here, in destination one. I am not supposed to be telling you this, but you're bound for destination two unless you change something starting tomorrow." After his grandmother told him this, her disappointment in him felt more painful than surgery.

"How can I earn my ticket for destination one back, Grandmother?" Rafael asked, but deep down, he had already assumed he knew the answer. *Rey*, Rafael thought in defeat, before his grandmother responded.

"If you are to be bound for destination one and not two, you must end that foolish wedding tomorrow. The Operator will not tolerate you giving your heart to the same sex," his grandmother replied. Rafael cried some more, but the tears were no longer for his grandmother.

"He gave me a kidney when he barely knew me," Rafael argued. "How could I hurt someone with such a good heart, with so much love?"

"Easy, think of your mother and father who gave you life," his grandmother finished.

Rafael woke up.

The next morning, Rafael showered, picked up his white suit, and wore it.

"And do you, Rafael Rosario, take Reyman Debroyi to be your husband until death do you part?" the marriage official asked.

Rafael looked around the church and saw that everyone awaited an answer.

"I...," Rafael began.

When he was ninety-five years old, Rafael Rosario finally received a call from the Operator. Rafael followed instructions to the magical trail rail, Trail Rail F, and was given his ticket. Until his train arrived, Rafael did not look at his ticket number. When the train finally arrived, it did not say number one nor did it say number two.

"I'm so sorry," Rafael said before train number three took him to his final destination.

8

Tales of Cold

After exiting the building, Alfonzo Ramos waited in the wheelchair for his friend, Jesse Ortiz. After Jesse, a friendlier individual than Alfonzo, finished saying goodbye to more than half of the members in their support group, he pushed the wheelchair to where he parked his 2020 black-and-red Jeep Grand Cherokee. When his wife passed away because of stage four breast cancer, Jesse did not have anyone to rely on to help him cope. When his daughter committed suicide, however, it drove Jesse to the pointy end of a cliff; and if not for Alfonzo, he would have dived off head first. To repay Alfonzo, Jesse offered to be his caretaker whenever the opportunity presented itself. With Alfonzo being handicapped, there was always an opportunity.

"I'll prepare dinner," Jesse told Alfonzo when they arrived at the small condo he forced Alfonzo to share with him.

Alfonzo sat on the couch as Jesse prepared dinner in the kitchen. The remote was on his lap, but he did not turn the television on. Instead, he did what he always did ever since they moved into the condo: He stared at the dark screen and reminisced about times of despair and regret.

* * * * *

"Mommy, why does the wolf and some people choose to act mean?" Alfonzo asked his mother after she finished reading *Little Red Riding Hood*. He was four years old, and ICE had not yet deported his parents back to the Dominican Republic.

"Because the cruel world we live in today is like a gigantic freezer. When you put a heart inside a freezer for way too long, it can either burst, stay strong enough to last till it is taken out, or it can adapt to the temperature and turn so cold it becomes ice. Adapting to the cold is easier than fighting it, and so most people pick that option."

At that time, Alfonzo had no idea what his mother meant by this, and so he just pretended he did.

When Alfonzo turned seven years old, two years after the deportation of his parents, he began to understand the cruelty his mother had spoken of. His Aunty Thalia, in whose care he was left, was never around, but her closeted husband Tommy was. Tommy was in his early thirties, but his age did nothing for Alfonzo whom he sexually abused not long after Alfonzo's arrival into their home.

"Come suck it," Alfonzo remembered Tommy saying. It was December 23, and it was cold outside. All he wanted to do was just color and imagine he was with his parents in the beautiful beaches of Hato Mayor, but the urges had kicked in for Tommy like no other days. Alfonzo remembered how much he hated how "it" tasted. Tommy was not a big fan of showers, and so the taste of sweat always bothered Alfonzo's mouth.

"I don't want to anymore. Don't make me," Alfonzo pleaded, but he knew Tommy well enough to know he was going to pay for disobeying. Tommy, when angry, reminded Alfonso of the angry wolf from *Little Red Riding Hood*. Tommy walked over to where Alfonzo sat on the rug and kicked him. Like a feather, Alfonzo flew off the rug and landed on his face.

"When Daddy say suck it, you need to fucking suck it!" Tommy said angrily before pulling Alfonzo's curly hair and forcing him to face his zipper. "I'll fucking kill you if you bite me!" Tommy threatened before he unzipped his pants and forced his penis inside Alfonzo's mouth.

An hour later, as Tommy slept in his room, Alfonzo contemplated running away. His aunty Thalia always told him about the disappearance of little kids, how an evil man who lives in the woods eats them like the wolf who craved the three little pigs. *He can't eat me,* Alfonzo thought. With his favorite sweater on, he sneaked out the window, into the cold winter night. Before Alfonzo opened the gate, Tommy opened the front door and spotted him.

"Get back here you little fucker!" Tommy yelled and ran toward him. Alfonzo took off and did not look back. A few blocks away from the house, Alfonzo slightly turned and saw Tommy was still on him. Alfonzo changed directions and ran into the scary woods. When Alfonzo was certain he was longer being followed, he stopped for a breather. For some reason, the woods had felt ten times colder than described in the stories he'd heard. When Alfonzo looked at the ground, he noticed something bizarre. *It does not snow in Florida,* Alfonzo thought. Alfonzo watched the color disappear in his palms, along with the rest of his body, and then collapsed on the bed of snow.

When Alfonzo woke up, he was in a cabin.

"Good morning, son. I am the demigod Adamis Orionis," a pale man said. He had dark, curly hair; amber eyes; and wore a complete gray uniform (suit, pants, and shoes). Alfonzo looked behind Adamis, and next to the log fireplace were five little kids who looked the same age as him.

"Are you going to eat me?" Alfonzo asked.

Adamis laughed, and the other kids joined in.

"No, silly. I was tasked with finding lost kids like you and bringing them to Tri-Rail F," Adamis said, and Alfonzo felt more confused. Alfonzo did not know what Tri-Rail F was or where it was.

"What is that?" Alfonzo asked.

"You're joking! Everyone knows about Tri-Rail F," one of the little girls replied before Adamis could answer. "My mommy tells me about the four magical trains every night and how they all go to magical worlds!" She placed her hands on her hips.

What a diva, Adamis thought. *Can't wait to see her reaction when she learns of her final destination.*

"Nuh-uh," a boy replied. "My mommy said the Operator has two tri-rails. One with four trains and the forbidden one with two trains numbered five south and north. She said he hid it because no one can survive there long enough to get on the train."

He looked at the little girl, and they had a staring contest. After the contest, all of the kids turned and looked at Adamis for the truth. Even Alfonzo could not take his eyes off Adamis.

"Yes, that tale is true," Adamis told the kids. "The Operator had two tri-rails and had to cast away one of them because the temperature surrounding that tri-rail became severely fatal, the forbidden tri-rail." Adamis's amber eyes locked into Alfonzo's eyes.

"But, sir, why did it become fatal?" the shortest boy in the room asked.

Adamis felt stuck. He vowed to never lie, but he knew he could not answer the question. "A curse placed by the Operator's sister long ago. Now, when we get to Tri-Rail F, pinky promise me none of you will sneak away from the herd and walk a mile-and-a-half past the train tracks of the four trains," Adamis said.

All the kids gathered around the mattress Alfonzo was lying on and pinky promised as a group.

Why tell us the exact mile if he does not want us to go there? Alfonzo wondered after his pinky promise. *I have to know.*

The next day, Alfonzo opened his eyes and found himself, along with the other kids, standing in a large grassy field.

"We're here. I traveled as you guys slept. Have your tickets ready 'cause the trains should arrive soon." Adamis told the kids and gave Alfonzo a smile. There were a bunch of other people waiting for trains. Alfonzo looked at his ticket, and it was marked "one," for train number one. Alfonzo waited for Adamis to give his attention to one of the kids and made a run for the train tracks.

"Ramos nooo!" Adamis screamed, but Alfonzo did not look back or stop.

Exactly as Adamis described, Alfonzo found a bush after walking for a mile-and-a-half away from the train tracks of Tri-rail F. Alfonzo entered the bush, and the world behind disappeared. Alfonzo found himself in a snowstorm. The cold Alfonzo experienced in the woods could not compare. The temperature of the woods felt like boiled oil compared to the snowflakes of the forbidden tri-rail as they fell on him. In agony, Alfonzo did a three hundred sixty degree turn and could not see anything but dense fog. Alfonzo cried, yelled for someone—anyone—to come save him, but nothing happened. No one, not even Adamis came. Alfonzo felt his heart begin to feel as if it would burst. He remembered what his mother told him; he remembered he had two other choices. "Anything but death." Alfonzo forced himself to say out loud and felt a painful response in his throat.

What felt like an eternity of waiting came to an end when Alfonzo heard the sound of an approaching train. *I did it,* Alfonzo thought. *I did the impossible.* A train marked "Number Five North" stopped in front of him. Inside the train, after Alfonzo felt the remaining tissues of his heart turn into ice, he took a deep breath and closed his eyes.

When Alfonzo opened his eyes again, as if he had dreamed the whole experience, he found himself in a hospital.

"Oh my god. Thank God you're okay. You could have died in those woods. Don't ever pull something like that ever again, Alfie!" Thalia told him, with Tommy next to her. Tommy had a sinister smile on his face.

"I'm sorry, Aunty," Alfonzo said.

With memories of Adamis and the forbidden tri-rail in the back corners of his mind, Alfonso obeyed every one of Tommy's desires until he turned fifteen. At fifteen, Alfonzo ran away and was recruited by a gang he only heard rumors of.

When he turned seventeen, Alfonzo knocked on Tommy's door a final time.

"Hello, Daddy. Let me in, or I blow your brains out. Not like old times!" Alfonzo said. He showed Tommy the car in the parking lot. It had three guys in the backseat and a driver. When Tommy looked back at him, Alfonzo showed him a pistol. Tommy opened the door and began to sweat.

"Suck it!" Alfonzo said when inside the house. Tommy kneeled down and unzipped Alfonzo's pants as fast as he could, but before he was able to put his mouth on Alfonzo's penis, Alfonzo pointed the gun at his head and pulled the trigger. *I chose cold,* Alfonzo thought, remembering his mother, as Tommy's body hit the marble floor.

9

Tales of Destiny's Poet

While it may not be worth it, sometimes we can't help but sacrifice too much for love. That is a sad tale I believe we are all bound to live, a truth that can only be learned through experience. For me, the price I had to pay to earn this valuable knowledge was imprisonment. My tale could be considered Karma's way of enacting revenge for my ancestors' beliefs and practices of slavery before 1804, or the time when I learned everything I thought was imaginary was actually just hidden, or a tale of true destiny, or the time I, Amelia Hilts, lived two lives, but only fell in love once.

Before I was Grace Lando, I was Amelia Hilts. The year was 1861. My husband, Joshua Pillson, and I lived in our beautiful two-bedroom house in the small village of Trevett in Boothbay, Maine. I never imagined being married to Joshua Pillson at the age of twenty-seven. Joshua and I first fell for each other in 1858. Joshua's entire family was a bunch of religious fanatics who believed in the whole "powerful man in the sky" mumbo jumbo. Joshua's father, Erick Linndol Pillson, was one of the two preachers at the church, but add to that the fact that he owned it.

My mom and Joshua's mother, Mrs. Pillson, grew up as best friends, and so my mom was dragged into their world. I hated the church, but my mom went every Sunday. She was committed. The only other person who attended more frequently than she was Erick himself.

In the beginning of 1858, rumors about the preacher's boy surfaced; people in town heard him sing for the first time and would not stop bragging about his angelic voice. I wanted to find out for myself. I started attending church with Mom. I'd sleep through the entire service, and as if I had an alarm in my mind, I'd wake up whenever Joshua stepped on the stage. This went on for three months.

One afternoon, I rode my bike to the woods, to be alone and draw, and learned my favorite hiding spot was hijacked. Before I said anything to the invader, he stood up—with a notebook and a pen in hand—and began to recite a poem.

It went something like this:

>Following stories of old,
>   In pursuit of gold,
> Through piles of rocks,
>   A rare light shines near.
>First came fear,
>   Although it was crystal, the mysterious light
>   remained unclear,
>   The light disappears,
>In my heart it reappears,
>   Beautiful, be happy, my dear.
>   Yes, it's true,
>   The rare diamond among rocks that uncrystallized my heart was, indeed, you.

When he finished, I froze. Joshua turned around. I did not hide. "I didn't think anyone actually came here," Joshua said. He seemed extremely nervous.

I knew what he meant. When we were growing up, the kids in town told a bunch of tall tales about the woods. If I believed them, I would have left town. "I knew you had a beautiful voice, but I had no idea you were such an aspiring poet," I told him. It made him less nervous. It made him smile, even, putting an end to the rumors that he never smiled.

From there, Joshua and I became close. Every afternoon, we met at the usual spot; he shared his poems, and in return, I shared my art. As he became a better poet, as I became a better artist, we became better lovers. Joshua was my first, and I his. My dad made many friends who had boys the same age as I, but none ever captured my heart the way the preacher's son did. What made it more special was that Joshua never forced any of the holy crap on me.

Then April 9, 1861, happened. Joshua and I had our very first real fight. "I cannot stand and watch children of God be treated like animals when there's something I can do to stop it!" Joshua said. It was the first time he ever raised his voice at me, probably the first time he had ever raised his voice.

"I forbid you to go!" I argued. I remember that night, I tried with great effort to hold back tears but failed.

"I can't expect you to understand because your family has a history of owning slaves. At the same time, you can't expect me not to join the Union!"

"No, I don't understand! If those niggers want ultimate freedom so badly, then they can surely fight for it themselves!"

Joshua stormed out of the house. He slept at his parents', but I saw him the next day.

"I just love you so much," I told him when we met at our special location. "I can't bear the thought of losing you for some helpless cause, but if you must go, then take this. Keep it on you at all times, and promise to come back to me.".

After he accepted the beautiful portrait I'd made of him days earlier, we cuddled in tears, as he hummed one of my all-time favorites of his songs.

His journey to war began that afternoon.

The battle of Fort Sumter happened on the twelfth, but after the moon smiled down upon us, on the eleventh, I biked to the woods. Desperation seized control of my body. One of the rumors I heard growing up was that, late after the moon shows, a magical well appears deep in the woods; and anyone lucky enough to discover it, with a coin present, would be given a wish from the keeper of the well.

I never knew the woods were so vast until that night. When I believed I was deep enough and did not see any magical well, I turned around to leave. Right before I left, however, I heard water dripping. I turned around and saw it—a magical well with glowing leaves of all colors all around it. I jumped forward and tossed the coin in, closed my eyes, and wished to be reunited with Joshua.

Seconds after my wish, she appeared. She was something out of another world. I never saw such mesmerizing features on any living being. "I am the goddess Isis, the keeper of this well, here to make your dreams a reality."

I almost bowed to her. The way her beautiful pale skin glowed set a high standard for the leaves of the magical wells. They could not compare.

"I already made my wish," I told her, and she smiled.

"Your participation is needed for it to come true. I have a set of tasks. After you obey them all, then you will be granted your wish. There is a magical tri-rail called Tri-Rail F. It is operated by a mystical being named the Operator. You will live till you turn ninety-five years old. Feel free to move on from Joshua in that time frame. The Operator will give you a call and a ticket when you arrive at Tri-Rail F for one of four trains. I want you to toss out the ticket, cross the train tracks, walking for a mile-and-a-half. You will discover the Operator's forbidden and long-forgotten tri-rail. Unlike the four other trains, the train in this tri-rail, number five, goes to two destinations, north and south. If you truly love Joshua, then you will outlive the fatal weather climate of the forbidden tri-rail until the train arrives. You will get on train number five south, and with a token signifying your love for Joshua in hand, you will remake your wish as soon as you step inside the train. After you're done, leave it to the token and me to reunite you with your love who is soon to meet his maker."

I could not find it in my heart to love another the way I loved Joshua, so for the remaining sixty-three years, I waited for the Operator to call. When he finally did call, I traveled to the given location, and from there, I did everything Isis told me to do. Every day for sixty-three years, I had kept the instructions in mind, and when it came time, it felt as if the information had been given to me the day before.

When I arrived at the forbidden tri-rail, I was trapped in a snowstorm. The snowflakes that fell on my skin were not like regular snowflakes; they could be compared to a million tiny, pointy saw blades cutting through my skin. Literally seconds after I felt my heart beating slower, I heard the sound of a train approaching. I prayed for the first time. I prayed that the approaching train was heading south. Surprisingly, my prayers were answered. Inside, I made my wish again. Everything went dark afterward.

* * * * *

In the 1990s, a few days before his wedding to a beautiful woman named Julia, twenty-seven-year-old Mauricio Rosario visited his best friend, twenty-five-year-old Grace Lando, whom he considered a sister from another mother and asked, "I wrote this beautiful poem for Julia. I want to add it to my vows. Do you like it?"

Before Grace gave an opinion, every memory of mine as Amelia Hiltz merged into her and made us one. After my subconscious seized control, I felt Grace's vanish. Grace, an African American woman of light skin tone had one thing in common with my former physique, the slimness. She was an extremely beautiful African American woman. I recognized the poem and immediately knew my wish was almost true. *What should I do now?* I wondered. As if Isis linked her mind to mine, I heard an echo telling me to kiss Mauricio.

"Joshua, how much do you love Julia?" I asked. Grace's memories stayed in my mind.

"Well, I don't know who Joshua is, but I don't think there's a girl better for me than Julia, even in another life. If you believe in all of that mumbo jumbo crap, I would have been with Julia. We were destined for each other."

And after Mauricio, formerly Joshua, said this, I felt I had lived those sixty-three years of heartbreak over again. *I had waited for so long,* I thought. One kiss and I could end the heartbreak finally. I walked to Mauricio and gave him a hug instead. A month after the wedding, I received a call from the Operator again. When I returned, I waited for the train numbered on my ticket. The first time, my ticket said train number two, but the second time, it said train number one. When the train arrived at its destination, a world full of magic beyond description, I stepped off and realized I was no longer in Grace's body. I was back into my own body but younger, as if the sixty-three years never happened. A day later, after swimming with magical mermaids, I returned to the island. I picked up some daisies, and when I stood back up, I found myself face-to-face with him.

"Joshua," I said.

10

Wishful Tales of Mass

The cold wind blew from the waves of the ocean and stopped at Frankie Storndon's smooth skin. His soft pale face took it all in. *This is the perfect place*, Frankie thought. He stood on the guard tower and looked up at the beautiful moon as the peaceful breeze touched his face. His father's gun aimed at his head, he was ready to pull the trigger. Frankie believed he had reached the point of no return. As Frankie focused his eyes on the shiny moon, he saw it all—what had brought him to the beach that night. It had all started the day Frankie got hired at Bru's Room. That was the event that led to his informal introduction to Massimo Luigini, someone Frankie never expected to love the way he had. In a nonromantic manner, Frankie considered Massimo to be one of his soulmates.

In January 2017, two years before, during his second day as a busser at Bru's Room, Frankie was told by the server who worked outside to bring water to a married couple. Before Frankie arrived with the water, the husband decided to use the restroom. Unexpectedly, as Frankie approached the lady with the water, he tripped. Frankie had quick reflexes, but he was only able to catch one of the glasses. The other had spilled all over the lady's breast.

"You can't fucking be serious!" was the first thing the angry lady yelled, loud enough to get everyone's attention. It did not end there though; the lady followed up by calling Frankie a retard, along with a slew of classroom insults that implied Frankie was the dumbest person she'd ever met.

Frankie stood there frozen. He did not know how to react with so many eyes gazing only at him. At the sight of the husband who returned from the bathroom, Frankie began to sweat.

"You should fucking be fired, moron!" the husband said after his wife explained what happened, so close to Frankie's face that his spit landed on the tip of Frankie's nose.

"Why don't you two privileged fucks go suck on some dicks? I can't tell which of you two is the bigger bitch!" someone at the next table said.

Like a turkey that spent three days in the freezer and then was put in a big bowl of hot water, Frankie felt himself thawing.

The gentleman who had spoken up walked from where he sat with a young lady and stood next to Frankie. The husband grew more pissed. Frankie knew the situation was only going to get worse, but he had no idea how to stop it. Frankie's rescuer gave a look and then grabbed the other glass of water from his tray, and before Frankie could react, he spilled it all over the husband.

A huge fight broke out. Frankie witnessed the first punch, taken by the husband, and then ran for staff members to help break up the fight. When he returned with help, the fight was at its peak, and to his surprise, no one attempted to stop it. Before they were separated and tossed out by the entire staff, Frankie took a good look at the two men and made the conclusion that the husband lost the fight. A broken nose, a black eye, and a messed-up jawline provided the evidence. This made Frankie's night.

On the thirteenth, the very next day, as if fate had something to do with it, Frankie decided to work out in the afternoon for the very first time since he signed up three months before. As Frankie finished his bicep curls, he saw the reflection of a familiar face walking by behind him. Frankie dropped the dumbbells and rushed to catch up to his rescuer.

"Thank you for last night. I am Frankie."

"Of course, dude. I'm Massimo." That introduction marked the beginning of a new brotherhood. Frankie had many workouts with Massimo and later learned that Massimo was a security guard at Johnnie Brown's, an outdoor bar with live rock performances that Frankie always visited after his weekend night studies at the nearby Starbucks. *He's going to be the best cop this world will ever have*, Frankie thought one night as he observed Massimo work. It was not because Massimo ranked first in the police academy the year he graduated; it was how Massimo treated the boy with Down syndrome who was always at the bar at the same time as Frankie. Frankie believed himself to have a good heart, but it was nothing compared to Massimo's. A bar full of people and Massimo was the only one who did not look at this boy as if he was unusual, a freak.

Usually when Frankie visited the bar, he stayed until they closed and then went out with Massimo after. Massimo's shift at the bar concluded at 2:00 a.m., but Frankie didn't mind.

In September of 2019, Massimo came to learn Frankie was homeless.

"How long?" Massimo asked after Frankie confessed.

"It's been two weeks," Frankie told him.

"To be honest with you, dude, if you weren't one of my best friends, I'd beat your ass. I'm telling you, you're welcome at my house," Massimo began. "You remind me of Rey. You guys are the same. You are both stubborn," Massimo finished, and Frankie felt sorry for him. Reyman Debroyi was Massimo's best friend. Massimo, Reyman, and Frankie went out for a good time once, before Reyman drove into a tree in an attempt to take his own life but instead ended up in a coma.

Massimo did not want to take no for an answer, and Frankie's neck was starting to hurt from sleeping in his car. Frankie agreed to stay with Massimo until things at his house worked themselves out.

September 3 was Massimo's twenty-third birthday, and even though he had to wake up early the next day for work, Frankie agreed to celebrate with Massimo until morning came. Massimo told him he was going to New York the next day. Frankie told Massimo he would be returning home on the fourth.

"Damn. You know you don't have to rush to go back so soon," Massimo told him, but Frankie hated to feel like a burden to his friend, even though he knew how much Massimo cared.

On October 29, 2019, Frankie overheard gossip of Massimo's death at the gym. Frankie did not want to believe it. Frankie hadn't heard or seen Massimo ever since September 4, but he assumed it was because Massimo was in New York, where he'd told Frankie he was going the night of his birthday. Frankie ran out of the gym and drove to Massimo's house, in a panic attack.

Frankie dialed Massimo's number four times. "Hey, Mass, it's Frank. Please call me back whenever you hear this," Frankie said outside Massimo's door after he'd knocked ten times and no one answered.

It wasn't until the thirty-first of October that one of the family members he reached out to on Facebook finally reached back to him.

"Yeah, Massimo took his own life on September 5," Kate, Massimo's cousin whom Frankie had only met once, told him.

"Please tell me it was not with the gun," Frankie forced himself to say, remembering the awesome feeling he felt when Massimo was showing him how to operate the gun the night of Massimo's birthday. *I held that gun*, Frankie thought. *Why let me hold a gun you planned on taking your life with, two days later?* Frankie did not know what to feel first. Feelings of sadness, regret, anger, and confusion battled for the empty spaces in his mind.

On November 5, after deciding he was tired of feeling all of it at once, unable to function, Frankie broke the lock to his father's room and stole his pistol, almost an identical one to the one Massimo used. Frankie thought of the beach at night, the best time and the most peaceful place for him to end all the pain he felt inside.

Before he pulled the trigger, Frankie heard the strangest thing, the crying of an infant coming from the waves of the ocean. Frankie dropped the pistol and ran toward the crying infant. It was dark, and he could not see anything; but after detecting where the sound was coming from, Frankie dove to the rescue, forgetting that he did not know how to swim. *If I am drowning, it will be after I save this baby,* Frankie thought right before a huge wave pushed him under. Before his eyes closed, Frankie felt the salty water go inside of him, as if he had drunk the entire ocean.

Frankie opened his eyes. He was no longer under the killer wave. Instead he was under a cave, with water that only came up to his knee. On the tallest rock in the cave, Frankie spotted the person who might have rescued him from drowning. "The baby. Did you save it?" Frankie asked, ignoring the tentacles that replaced legs on the beautiful girl who lay on the rock.

"I am the goddess Anahi Ta. You are hurting, and my master, the Operator, sent me to help you heal. I was the baby. This is for you." And the young girl pulled something from under the water. It was a notebook with a pencil attached to its cover.

Frankie was confused. He did not want to believe he was stuck in a dream but remembered he grew up in a household where tall tales were more welcome than facts. Frankie walked closer to the rock and accepted the notebook.

"Your act of selflessness earned you this. You recently lost someone you loved and you need clarity, and this notebook can help you. You have a whole day to use it, and it can do anything except bring back the dead. Use wisely."

Though it felt like a scene from Aladdin, too good to be true, Frankie gave in to his desperate need for answers. The beautiful young girl with tentacles for legs disappeared after Frankie opened the blank notebook and began to write.

"In my dream, we met again." Frankie wrote down on the first line. Smoke surrounded him, and he no longer was in a cave. Frankie was back to Bru's Room. The year was 2017 again, and everyone was gone, except the bartender.

"Massimo?" Frankie asked.

The bartender turned around, and it was Massimo.

"Margarita," Massimo said and put a coaster in front of Frankie.

"Fuck the drink. Why?" Frankie said after putting the notebook and the pencil down.

"We don't have time for why. I think we should use this time for us to enjoy each other's company one final time." Massimo sat the drink on the coaster.

"I am sad, confused, and angry all at once," Frankie said, with the first sip of his drink.

"Why? Start with sad," Massimo demanded.

"I am sad because the world, that poor down syndrome boy, and I lost such a great guy. I am confused because you never once seemed unhappy. And I am angry because I must've been a horrible and selfish friend if you couldn't call me in such a time of need." Ignoring the tears that fell in the glass, Frankie finished the entire drink on the second sip.

"No. You were not. I love you and everyone else I did not call." Massimo replied and then placed his arm on Frankie's shoulder. "Now," Massimo said, walking from behind the bar, "we made plans to visit New York together. Use that magic notebook of yours, and take us there."

Frankie obeyed. He grabbed the notebook and pencil and wrote, "Massimo and I visited New York. We visited Central Park, enjoyed its many attractions together, and then we ended on the beach back home, ready to watch the sunset."

"Time's almost up," Frankie told Massimo later that day and felt a pain in his heart.

"This whole day was great. Let me write down your last request," Massimo suggested, and Frankie could not find it in himself to deny the last request of a dead man, a dead man he loved. Frankie handed Massimo the notebook and pencil.

"I love you, dude," Massimo told him before he wrote, "And Frankie never tripped and spilled water on that lady, therefore never met me."

The sun finally set, as smoke surrounded Frankie and Massimo.

On September 5, 2019, after one of Frankie's study sessions, he decided to see what Johnnie Brown's was about. Usually he just walked by, but that night, they were playing "Carry on Wayward Son," a favorite of his. Frankie knew he had to stop by. He sat down at a table to watch the band. A server approached and gave him a drink menu. Before he told her what he wanted, a fight between two drunk guys broke out. "Whoa," Frankie said.

"I know. We only have one guard on the clock tonight, so it's hard for him to manage all the drunk heads," the server said. Frankie was curious and asked the server why they only had one guard. Usually, when he walked by, there were two.

"Well, this morning, our other guard's mom called and told us he took his own life," she told him. Frankie could not explain it, but he felt a sudden pain in his heart after he heard this. He did not even know the person.

"What was his name?" Frankie asked the server, and she told him it was Massimo Luigini.

"My condolences," he told her and then changed his mind about the drink.

11

Tales of the Fifth Night

Askari Fazil was never a believer of magic until he laid eyes on Rafa Qadir. Though the hijab did a fantastic job at hiding most of Rafa's body, it could not hide her beauty or the kindness that existed in her heart. When he first met her, he had no idea she had long dark-brown hair, which could be perceived as midnight black from a distance. But he was certain her unique blue-green eyes were Allah's inspiration for the beautiful sea, the marvelous plants, and full moons. That is, if there was an Allah. Askari spent days on the street, playing his kora for passengers, for necessities before he crossed paths with Rafa.

"Would you play for me?" she asked him. He could not imagine a world where he would deny such a beautiful creature the opportunity to enjoy one of his beloved tunes. She did not know anything about him, but it did not stop her from offering him a place in her father's large home after she heard him play. Though Rafa's father turned Askari away at first, it did not stop the developing friendship between Askari and Rafa. After many fights with her father, Rafa was allowed to invite Askari to have dinner with the family. The friendship became more. The love that existed between Askari and Rafa became so vibrant that it eventually touched the heart of Rafa's father who could not help but to agree to letting Askari move in with them. Rafa always planned to go to the country of dreams, America, to become a doctor, and when Askari heard of this, it broke him into a million pieces. However when her father saw how destroyed Askari was by the news of her departure, he included Askari on the route he had established for her, on the condition that he would marry her as soon as they arrived and promised to always put her first. As promised, three years after their arrival in America, they had a traditional American wedding.

Life continues to throw curveballs at me, Rafa thought after losing her job. "It was almost impossible to find a job that did not require papers, and now what?" she complained to Askari a few months after their wedding. She had first learned that her father had lost all his assets back home and then found out she could not have kids—two facts that broke both her heart and Askari's.

Askari, speechless after she told him, sought to comfort her. "We will survive with my job," he reassured her, remembering the promise he had made to her father to always put her first.

One night, after he closed the corner store he worked at and walked to his car, he looked across the street and saw an elderly Native American woman and a child who could not have been older than three, sleeping at the bus stop. After a sound of thunder nearly made him deaf, Askari knew he could not go home and sleep peacefully under his not-so-perfect roof without helping them the best way he could.

"I know you guys don't know me, but I work in the corner store across the street. It will rain soon. I can adjust the heater so you guys can sleep in there instead. You have to promise to leave before nine thirty. If my boss finds out, then he'll fire me," Askari said.

The elderly woman looked at Askari and then at the little girl. The little girl nodded her head, and they stood up. Askari opened the door and let them inside, and less than a minute later, it began to pour outside.

"The world still has kind hearts. You must have kids, no?" the elderly woman asked Askari as the little girl looked for a comfortable spot to lie.

"No. My wife and I can't have kids. Well, she can't have kids. I love her to death though," Askari replied as he adjusted the heater to be warmer.

"I'll go home and get pillows and blankets. I don't live too far." Askari ran out into the rain and rushed home. When he told his wife why he was taking their only spare blankets and pillows, she kissed him and told him he was sweet.

Askari returned with the blankets and pillows. After the little girl fell fast asleep, the elderly woman asked Askari to sit down for two minutes. Askari obeyed and sat down as close as he could, out of respect for an elderly.

"Have you ever heard the tales of the fifth night?" she asked him.

Before he could respond, his confused face exposed him.

"Legend has it, if you bring a serpent and kill it at a deserted crossroads on the fifth night of the month, then a beautiful man will greet you and give you one thing your heart desires most. Say children," the elderly woman told Askari before Askari forced himself to leave. The elderly woman and the child were gone the next morning, but Askari spent the entire month contemplating about the fifth night. By the second day of the next month, December, Askari decided he was going to find a serpent.

After the moon kissed the sun good night, on the fifth night of December, Askari stood in the middle of the closest deserted crossroads he knew, with a bloody knife in hand and a dead serpent near his foot and waited.

"I am the demigod Adameous Orionis. Tell me what your heart desires most, and prick your finger with this," Adameous said and gave Askari a needle. The needle was not like any Askari had ever seen; it was a small ball with three points. Before Askari asked him which of the three points he needed to prick his finger, Adameous gazed at the middle point. *I could wish for wealth. Rafa and I would be set*, Askari thought, *but she and I have always wanted a child.*

"But if you ask for five children, fate will also guarantee you unimaginable wealth," Adameous said, "a two-for-one deal."

It frightened Askari. *How did he know what I was thinking?* Askari thought and reminded himself where he was and how he got there. "Why five?" Askari asked.

"Why not?" Adameous responded.

Askari felt too terrified to argue.

"There are other serpents bleeding to death, so let's make this faster!" Adameous yelled. After he pricked his finger, with no blood present, Askari remembered something his wife Rafa always said. "Everything in life requires payment, good and bad alike." He was still terrified, but Askari asked Adameous about the price for his wish.

"When the last of the five children turns ten, you will bring your least favorite here on the fifth of the month and sacrifice him or her in front of me, with the same knife you used to kill the serpent."

After Adameous told him this, Askari found himself alone at the crossroads with no further explanation. There was no serpent or knife; there was only a bottle of something that looked like apple juice. Askari had seen enough fictional movies to know his wife needed to drink the magic potion if she wanted to bear children. The next day, Askari discreetly poured the magic potion into Rafa's coffee. Nine months later, Askari and Rafa welcomed quintuplets. Two girls and three boys whom they named Aida, Aisha, Ajmal, Akeem, and Anivens. It was Rafa's idea to start all their names with the same letter, and Askari did not fight it.

When Askari and Rafa celebrated the first birthday of the quintuplets, it reminded Askari of what he had to do when they turned ten years old. After his meeting with Adameous, Askari searched for other tales like the fifth night until he came to know about a fortune teller named Madam Ibiza. He heard she was a mystic older than time itself and knew the answers to all of life's greatest questions.

"I'm stuck," Askari told Madam Ibiza when he finally found her site of operation and explained his crossroads dilemma to her.

"Maybe if I tell you the future of your five children, then your choice will be easier to make. Imagine the loss if you sacrifice the one who's destined to bring you wealth," Madam Ibiza told him.

Askari agreed to let her tell him the future of his five children. *Maybe it is a trick, and the demigod just wants to make a fool of me by having me kill the one who could bring the most wealth*, Askari thought before he gave Madam Ibiza permission to glimpse the future of his five children.

"Wow. It's obvious now. You must sacrifice the last child. Anivens," Madam Ibiza told Askari after an interaction with her crystal ball.

Anivens is the only one who asks me about work, Askari thought, *the only one who won't sleep until he knows I am home and safely in bed, the only one who cooks for me when I say I am hungry, and even though the meals are always disgusting, they always fill me.*

"How can I sacrifice Ani when he has the kindest heart of all my children?" Askari asked Madam Ibiza, and without his consent, she told him more.

"Aida will become the richest investment banker of her time. Aisha will be the greatest singer of her time. Ajmal will become a doctor. Akeem will marry a monarch, making him a king of England. Anivens will bring about the death of you and your wife."

After Madam Ibiza told him this tragic fate, Askari begged her to go into details, but no matter how much more money he offered, she refused and kicked him out instead.

Anivens's kindness toward his father did not change, but when he turned ten years old, Askari asked him to go on a little adventure. As he was ordered to, Askari, with a broken heart, brought Anivens to the same crossroads. Adameous appeared with the knife and placed it in Askari's hand. Askari looked Anivens in the eyes and told him, "I love you more than life itself, but this had to be done for the sake of your mom and your brothers and sisters." He pushed the knife inside. Before the knife reached Anivens's heart, it disappeared, along with the wound it had already created.

"A father should never have a favorite child or be willing to sacrifice one no matter the circumstances. My father is bound to suffer in an endless fire for eternity because my grandfather had a favorite," Adameous said. He turned Askari around, made sure there was direct eye contact, made the knife reappear, and pushed it inside till he was convinced it had reached Askari's heart.

Though traumatized, Anivens ran back home with soaked eyes after Adameous disappeared and told of his father's demise. No one believed him when he told them how it happened.

Three months later, Rafa's broken heart gave out. Her final thought was she could not imagine her heart functioning without the oxygen that it needed for pumping blood, and that was Askari.

12

Tales of Lover's Curse

When Lisa Jones saw them walk into the lobby, they were only strangers. *Who could have predicted the two guys who checked into room 202 H, Alfonzo Ramos and Betronio Olson, would have turned into heroes? Those big arms of his,* she thought, referring to Alfonzo's arms.

"We were in the process of saving ourselves and heard screams," Alfonzo told her later, "We made the best of a tragic incident."

Lisa felt lucky and was grateful. Alfonzo could have saved anyone on the second floor from the mysterious fire and decided to save her. Lisa walked over and offered to repay Alfonzo Ramos, but he refused. This happened three months before Lisa moved in with her fiancée, Claudia, three months before the dreams started.

"Tishan, do Haitians have folklores about dreams?" Lisa asked her coworker, Tishan Lu'sent, whom she had met and become friends with in middle school. It was Tishan who'd helped her get a job at the library as a receptionist.

"Girl, too many," Tishan said and wheeled her chair closer. "Have you been having creepy dreams?"

"You know I don't do superstitions. That's your thing. I've been having the same weird dreams for almost four months now. They feel too real to be dreams," Lisa told Tishan, as she focused on the kids playing on the nearby rug.

"Tell me about this dream," Tishan suggested.

Lisa had not told anyone, not even Claudia, but she knew she could trust Tishan. Tishan had never betrayed her trust. "Ever since the fire, I've been having these dreams about the guy who carried me out. I am more lesbian than Ellen DeGeneres, but these dreams contradict that," Lisa said.

Tishan did not find what Lisa was describing uncommon. She'd heard many stories about dreams and the different meanings of each. "I know a fortune teller named Madam Ibiza. I'll send her over. She believes plants connect you to the world and its history, so brew her some tea and pay her fairly and she'll help you understand your dreams," Tishan said and walked over to remove a kid from the top of the kid's snack table.

Lisa thought about the offer for three days. On the fourth day, Lisa called Tishan and agreed to meet with Madam Ibiza. Madam Ibiza was at Lisa's front door after sunset. Lisa asked Madam Ibiza to come in, but she declined and insisted on the two sitting in the backyard instead. Madam Ibiza allowed Lisa to describe the dreams as she sipped her tea before making a conclusion.

"They're not dreams. They're memories of a prior incident of yours forcing themselves up due to a curse placed a very long time ago," Madam Ibiza said bluntly.

Lisa almost laughed but forced herself not to. She did not want to offend Madam Ibiza in any way. "Entertain me. Since I am paying you to be here," Lisa replied. She waited for Madam Ibiza to tell her a bogus story like the many she'd heard from Tishan in the break room.

"Once upon a time, in the French region formerly known as Gevaudan, a hunter named Aubert Bartholome, while hunting a wild boar, laid his eyes on the second most beautiful girl he'd ever seen. She had with her a basket covered by a table linen. Aubert, who grew up alone, mostly in the woods, did not know how to approach the beautiful girl and talk to her. When Aubert saw he was about to lose the girl, he did the first thing he could think of. He approached and pleaded for a piece of bread from her basket.

"Le destine ne m'a pas favorise' aujourd'hui" (fate had not favored him that day), Aubert told the beautiful girl, before he showed her his empty sack and bow and arrows. The girl told Aubert it was not bread that was covered in the basket and that her house was not too far from the woods if he wanted to join her for supper. Aubert, on the way to the girl's house, finally asked for her name.

"Je m'appelle Celine," she told him. After eating, the girl asked Aubert if he wanted to spend the night, and Aubert accepted. One night turned into too many to count, and before Aubert knew it, he was married to Celine, and she was seven months pregnant with his child. By the seventh month, rumors, which had been going on way before Aubert met Celine, increased—rumors of a witch amongst the villagers who stole children and took them deep into the woods to sacrifice them to the demigod, Adameous, for health and beauty. The villagers gathered together after one reported seeing Celine in the woods and took her to be burned at the stake.

Aubert, deep in his heart, knew his wife was incapable of committing such crime and was determined to prove her innocence before they burned her with his unborn child. Aubert had one true suspect in mind, Dariela, the most beautiful and mysterious woman he ever laid eyes on. As far as Aubert knew, Dariela was the only one who lived deep enough in the woods, away from the village.

Aubert visited the cabin, and when Dariela left, he searched for anything that could connect her to the missing children. When he did not find any, he came back at a later time and planted some. Kids' shoes, clothes, and the names of all the missing kids written on a notebook were all found in the cabin when Aubert returned with the villagers the very next morning. Celine was given back to Aubert, and Dariela was to be burned at the stake instead.

"S'il vous plait, mon enfant a seulement trois ans," Dariela cried to the villagers, telling them her child was only three years old, and that she would never kill little children ("Je ne tuerais jamais les petits enfants.")

The villagers, without any remorse, set the fire. She screamed and looked down and saw who was responsible. Before the fire took all of her, Dariela looked into Aubret's eyes and cast a curse, a curse that would allow Aubert and Celine to live many lives. In each life, they would always meet and fall in love, and after they had a kid together, the kid would die tragically, and they would remember their previous lives and the witch.

"So who was sacrificing the kids?" Lisa asked Madam Ibiza after she told her the story, "and what does it have to do with me?"

"Well, you are Celine in this life, and in your life before this, you were Jackie Bernes and lived in Maine. She got into a bad car accident and lost her memory, and when she grew tired of feeling lost to the people who claimed they loved her, she searched for ways to regain her memory. Jackie heard of a magical well that granted wishes, and she journeyed deep into the woods in her town in search of it. Jackie found it and wished to have all her memories back. What she did not expect was to get memories back from all those previous cursed lives. The memories pained Jackie for a long time and nearly made her insane until she heard of *Tales of the Fifth Night*. Jackie had discovered a way to break the curse.

On the fifth night of July, as the tale suggested, Jackie murdered a serpent and was greeted by the demigod Adameous, and she told him she wished to be born a lesbian in her next life so that she does not fall for a man. The dreams you've been having come from her second wish, trying to reenact or break the curse. You're a lesbian as Jackie wished, and if you do not give in to the dreams you've been having about Alfonzo, who's really Aubert in this lifetime, and marry Claudia, then you will forget everything you know about the curse, and it will be broken. If you give in, the cycle continues."

"I see," Lisa said. Lisa visited her brother, Bohen Jones, and asked him for his input after she told him of her dilemma.

"Pretend you believe in all of it. What should I do?" Lisa asked her brother. Lisa knew Bohen was the most honest person she ever met; it was why she came out to him before anyone else, not because he was her brother.

"The story has many plot holes, but I think Aubert was sacrificing those poor children, not Celine or the other chick. You and Claudia have a great thing, so don't let fiction ruin it. Marry her," Bohen said.

Lisa agreed.

Two months after her meeting with Madam Ibiza, a memory lost deep in her mind, Lisa married Claudia. The two heroes who saved her in the fire, Betronio Olson and Alfonzo Ramos attended the wedding. *This is the beginning of a great friendship*, Lisa thought and smiled at the boys.

13

Tales of Syndrome's Last Dance

The sky was dark, marked for rain. Bohen Jones stepped out of the car with the gift basket and rushed up the steps. *I can't believe it's been a whole year*, Bohen thought and remembered the last time he saw Tishan. It was two days before his first flight on his world travels.

"Bring Tishan a gift basket from Montreal please. She's been bugging me to tell you," Bohen's sister told him over the phone two nights before his return. After the fourth ring, Bohen admitted Tishan was not home. He peeked through the windows and saw an empty living room. When Bohen stepped down and turned to leave, that's when he heard it. The music that was playing was familiar.

Maybe someone is home, Bohen thought. Discreetly, Bohen peeked through the wooden fence and saw her. *Whoa*, he thought, as she flew through the air like a passerine in search of liberation of some sort, with her eyes completely shut. The only time Bohen had ever witnessed someone dancing so passionately was before his father's unexpected death. *If gravity was not so heavy, this wingless angel would touch the heavens using just her tippy toe*, Bohen thought, *such a miraculous dancer*. Suspecting she was about to look in his direction, Bohen turned and walked toward his car. *Maybe Tishan moved*, Bohen thought as he rushed back to the car.

"Tishan was not home. But I saw this young lady dancing in the backyard. I have never seen anyone dance like that. Who is she?" Bohen asked his sister, Lisa Jones, over the phone, on his way back.

"Oh, you're talking about Aisha. I thought Tishan told you about them. She took them in after Askari and his wife died because she didn't want them to live in the street or be in the foster system," Lisa told him.

Bohen felt confused. Askari had worked for him for years in his corner store and never mentioned he had kids. When Bohen heard of Askari's death, overseas, the news broke his heart, but no one mentioned anything about any kids.

"I never knew Askari even had kids," Bohen told Lisa. Bohen never had an employee who came close to Askari. Though Bohen knew there was a line that employee and employer were to never cross, he always told Askari how much he appreciated him and how hard he worked and even asked him to join him for dinner a few times. *I guess he did not like me as much as I liked him*, Bohen told himself, *at least not enough to tell me about his personal life*.

Lisa went on, telling Bohen that Aisha's true gift was not her dancing but instead her singing. "When she sings, it's like heaven is on earth. She's remarkable," Lisa explained.

Bohen called Tishan the next day and begged her to let the kids have Thanksgiving at his house with him and Lisa, but she told him she was not working and was planning a big family dinner. Though he did not get his chance to formally meet the kids on Thanksgiving, luck was still on his side. Two days later, his employee, Sedrick, the man who had replaced Askari, walked over to Bohen on the cash register and whispered something in his ear.

"Take over here. I'll deal with them," Bohen said and walked to aisle three. Sedrick had complained to Bohen over the phone for weeks about shoplifters, and Bohen's chance had finally come to catch them red-handed. There was no way he was going to miss the opportunity.

"Miss, you haven't paid for that, so it shouldn't be going in your brother's book bag," Bohen said when he walked up to his smugglers. They jumped and in the process dropped the bag of chips and Hershey bars. When they turned around, it almost made Bohen jump too. *Damn*, Bohen thought, *I did not see that one coming.*

"Outside now!" Bohen demanded and led the way. With the two of them closely behind him, Bohen left through the back exit.

"Names?" Bohen asked.

"I am Aisha, and that's my brother Ajmal. He only agreed to do it because of me, so put me in trouble and not him," the miraculous bird Bohen had seen reaching for the heavens said, beating her brother to it.

"I know Tishan would be pissed off to hear about this, so let's work something out," Bohen said. Aisha and Ajmal, at the mention of their adopted mother's name, looked more terrified. Bohen smiled on the inside when he saw how easily it was to bait them. When they seemed ready for negotiation, Bohen went for the kill.

"You two allow me to treat you to a nice dinner at my place tonight in return for my silence," Bohen told them, and it surprised them more than when he caught her putting the snacks in his bag. After work, Bohen accessed Youtube on the television and played what he had watched earlier that month.

"It is almost that time of the year again. It is November 21, which means the 15th Annual Global Fantasee entry list is now open. So get out and show us your sparks, young talents!" Jerry Perkens said. He was Bohen's least favorite E! News reporter, mostly because Bohen could not see him as more than just a fan-programmed rat.

"That is correct. But, Jerry, let's talk about what our reigning champion, Ariana Grames said last night on the radio. Do you think she still has it?" Aniseka Oc'blee asked.

"Yes, Anise. Last night our reigning champ who's still being bashed by critics after her two recent performance mishaps had this to say to the radio: 'For those of you saying I am too old to be in this industry and that I should just admit it and retire, try to remember that I won the Annual Global Fantasee five years in a row. Here's the deal, if any of your current stars or newbies stop me from winning it for the sixth time, then I will release one last album and retire.'

"Listen, stars and newbies, one of you might not only take home fame and four million dollars but also the title of the person who ended the career of the biggest icon of her time!" Jerry finished.

When Aisha and Ajmal arrived, Bohen's meal was ready. He rewound the program before he opened the door.

"We steal because we feel like a burden whenever we ask Tishan for money or anything," Ajmal explained, on the couch, after Bohen asked them. Aisha agreed with him.

"You guys should not feel that way. Tishan is great. Anyway, do either of you sing or dance?"

Ajmal pointed at Aisha, who began to blush.

Bohen questioned Aisha about her taste in music, and when he was done, he asked her about her favorite singer. Bohen was disgusted when she told him her favorite singer was Ariana Grames herself, someone who broke Bohen's heart and made him unable to trust any woman again.

"She's not old and will win for the sixth time in a row to prove it," Aisha said, and it almost made Bohen vomit.

"But what if you could perform against her?" Bohen suggested.

Aisha and Ajmal turned away from the television and gave Bohen their attention.

"Beat her even," Bohen added, and Aisha was intrigued.

"I've seen you dance, Aisha, and I am confident you can win. I am willing to give you the four grand you need to enter this competition," Bohen said.

"I love dancing, but it's not my passion. I feel like I am destined to be a great singer one day. That's what I want to do," Aisha replied.

"Yeah, I know how great you can sing, but we have to approach this with dancing. I am not telling you to give up your dreams. The competition is in March, and there's no way you'll find a singing coach at a reasonable price to get you ready, but I know a great dance coach who's willing to work for free," Bohen said.

"Who?" Ajmal asked.

"Me. I haven't told anyone this, but I am dying. Helping you will be the legacy I leave behind," Bohen said.

Ajmal and Aisha thought of their dad, and both began to cry.

"But there are rarely dancers in the competition. Entering as anything but a singer is practically suicide," Aisha argued, as her tears fell on her plate. Her heart ached for Bohen, but she could not understand why he was not as sad as she was.

"Let's change that. Convince Tishan to let us go to New York. We'll make you the first dancer to ever win and the person to end the career of a music icon. Once the spotlight is shining on you, you will surprise the world with your beautiful singing," Bohen told them.

Aisha and Ajmal rushed home after dinner, with the gift basket Bohen had prepared, and told their siblings and Tishan the news. Tishan was more than happy to say yes to the idea, but she only allowed Ajmal to go with Aisha, forcing their other three siblings to stay behind.

On the plane to New York, Aisha asked Bohen how he learned to dance, and Bohen told them the story of his dad, a story only his sister, Lisa, knew.

"Global Fantasee was called something else when I was little. I bugged my father about entering, and when he grew tired of it, he took me to the beach and told me he had heard me. My father told me to just watch him, and I did. He danced the most beautiful dance I had ever seen. I was shocked because I did not know he was a great dancer. My father then said if I could do one of the moves he made, then he would teach me how to dance like him.

"I attempted to and landed face-first on the sand. He taught me to dance anyway. The competition was being held in California. My father bought four tickets. When my mom tried to wake him up the morning of the flight, my father never woke up. I stopped dancing that day, but I never lost the skill." After he finished, Bohen turned to look at the outside view so Aisha and Ajmal did not see the tears rolling down his cheek.

"My father died of Creutzfeldt-Jakob disease. Turns out dancing was not all he had to offer me," Bohen continued when they stepped off the plane. "He passed it down to me, and it's only been getting worse."

"Your daughter. Is that how she died too?" Ajmal asked.

The question took Bohen by surprise. He wondered how Ajmal knew and then remembered Lisa and Tishan talked about everything, perks of them being best friends. *Tishan must've told him*, Bohen told himself.

"Well, I sent my baby to school, and it turns out one of the other kids had enterovirus, D68. My daughter was infected, and her weak immune system made matters worse. The doctor said that the virus was not fatal, but I guess it was." Bohen broke down in tears. That time, there were no airplane windows to protect him.

Both Ajmal and Aisha hugged him. Aisha, who knew the tragic stories of the dead girl's mother, decided it was the wrong time to bring it up and did not. But later, in their hotel room, she told Ajmal the mother had left her daughter because the child was born with Down syndrome, a story Tishan had shared with her.

Aisha felt intimidated in her first practice, mostly because Bohen had shown her that dancing to him was like learning to ride a bicycle. *Maybe there's a chance for me after all*, she told herself, as she watched him move across the empty dance studio they'd rented. He looked like a plane that could fly, effortlessly, for millions of years without ever running out of fuel.

"You're good. You put Chris Brown to shame," Ajmal told Bohen when it was Aisha's turn to attempt to try what he showed her.

"Chris Brown is trash and does not know how to dance," Bohen joked and then kicked Ajmal out of the studio.

"I hear this year holds the record for the most entries. I can't wait for tomorrow!" Jerry Perkens said on the television on the twenty-fourth night of March. It nearly sent Aisha into a panic attack.

In round one of the competition, Aisha stepped on the stage and greeted the five judges.

"What's your nickname?" Katlyn Ross, the oldest of the judges, asked Aisha.

Aisha knew about her. She was named the most cutthroat individual in television history. "Syn…Syndrome," Aisha stuttered and to her surprise received a smile. Aisha could not remember the last time she saw Katlyn Ross smile. It boosted Aisha's confidence, at least a little.

"Dancing is like committing suicide here, but I think I speak for all the judges when I say that you are moving to round two, Miss Syndrome," Katlyn said after all the judges voted on Aisha's first performance.

By June 7, the competition was being discussed on almost all television networks. It was the biggest and most talked about to date, and part of the reason was that the four finalists, for the first time in history, included a dancer. By then Aisha had confessed to Bohen why she nicknamed herself Syndrome for the competition. "I know that your daughter had Down syndrome and that her mother left you guys because of it," Aisha said and expected Bohen to be mad, but instead it made him more determined to help her make history. Bohen did not reveal to Aisha that the infamous mother from the story was her archrival in the competition, the woman whose career she was there to end, the woman who nicknamed herself TearsNotCry for the competition.

Bohen kept himself out of the spotlight for the entire competition, but after Aisha shocked the entire world by earning a score of 32, defeating her semifinal rival who earned a score of 31.8, Bohen could not help himself but rushed to hug her on stage, dragging Ajmal behind him.

"This must be the mysterious coach you always talk about," Katlyn said, and the entire stadium began to applaud. "Thank you for coaching such a miracle dancer and for bringing her to us." She gave Bohen a smile.

After Bohen realized what he had done, he searched the entire stadium, and his eyes met those of the person he meant to avoid. When Bohen's eyes landed on Ariana's, as they had the first time he met her at the bar, every reason he ever had for despising her rushed back to his mind. The feelings increased when Ariana, TearsNotCry, earned a score of 40 in her semifinal, which the judges called the greatest performance of her music career.

On June 10, the whole world sat on the edge of their seats and paid close attention.

"TearsNotCry, please tell us the name of your final act and why you chose it," Katlyn said.

Next to the stage, Bohen stood next to Ajmal and Aisha, who began to sweat. After one look at Bohen, the woman he once gave his heart to began to cry for the first time since leaving him.

"My final act is called Beautiful Syndrome," she began, and it brought Bohen back to the hospital when he lied to his daughter about her mother and reminded him of when his daughter was fatally ill, when he had to be there for her all alone, and watching her die without ever having met her mother.

"During one of my vacations, I fell in love with that kindhearted man over there. We had a baby, and she was born with Down syndrome, and I abandoned them because of it. I valued my music reputation more. She's dead now, but this is for her," Ariana said before she began to sing. The entire stadium, judges included, froze until she finished the song.

After everyone eventually unfroze, Aisha still could not move a limb. Aisha could not tell if this was because judge Katlyn announced that Ariana, TearsNotCry, had scored 85 on her performance, passing the record-holding score of 75 or by the fact that Bohen had lied to her.

"I am done. I can't do this!" Aisha yelled and pulled away from Bohen outside the stadium.

"You're on in five, so pick yourself up!" Bohen said.

"You lied to me," Aisha said, but Bohen could see in her eyes that was not what was really convincing her to give up.

"Yeah, I did, but you came this far, so be mad at me after you're famous," Bohen told her.

"Yeah right. She just scored a record-breaking score. No dance move of mine can beat that," Aisha argued, and it lit something in Bohen's mind.

"Then sing. No rule says you can't change acts this late." Bohen knew it was a desperate move because he never actually heard Aisha sing, but he trusted his sister, Lisa, enough to believe. After Aisha agreed, Bohen held her and walked her up the stage. Bohen sat next to Ajmal on the front row and prepared to be amazed.

"Name of last act and what inspired it," Katlyn said.

"My coach suggested I switch acts and sing now, but I won't do that because I believe this will be the greatest dance performance he and the world will ever see. I call this one Arian's Last Dance. Arian was the name of my coach's daughter who died." Aisha handed over the mic and waited for the lights to be dimmed.

From the front row, Bohen watched a beautiful angel with feathers blue as the ocean, neon green as the heavenly trees that only the lucky few get to dream about descend from the sky, in a dancing manner, to rescue a young girl born with Down syndrome. After the rescue, the angel, on one tippy-toe and with closed eyes, defied gravity, and flew the girl to heaven. When the lights came back on, the entire stadium jumped up on their feet to clap and cheer.

"Syndrome, you scored 89!" Katlyn said.

Bohen watched, as Ajmal, the first to get on the stage, lifted his sister through the air to show her off to the crowd. Both had tears of joy running down their cheeks. Ajmal and Aisha made eye contact and asked for Bohen to join them on stage.

"This is your moment. Enjoy it," Bohen mouthed and smiled before the loud screams of the stadium faded into nothing and before Bohen's eyes slowly began to close.

When Bohen opened his eyes again, the stadium was empty, the lights were turned off, and everyone was gone. Bohen stood up to leave, and his phone began to ring.

"Hello," Bohen answered.

"Bohen, I am the Operator. I think you would agree that the time to be reunited with your daughter is now."

14

Tales of Cheater's Wish

I sat on train number two quietly until the guy who sat next to me asked, "What tragic event was about to take place in your life before the Operator called you?"

I told him my story from the beginning, the injustice that destroyed me, told it to a stranger whose name I did not bother to know. This tale of destruction and deception began with a rivalry. It was the first time I ever took a course with Eve Jackson, the high school cheerleader I was fortunate enough to fall in love with in my high school sophomore year. I avoided picking the same class with Eve for reasons that are not to be discussed until I accidentally took a course with her in college. We attended the University of South Carolina. My major was biological and biomedical science, and Eve's was theology and religious studies. Eve learned I was not the only familiar face in English 200 on the first day of class. We were taking creative writing, voice, and community. Cole Reed, Eve's archnemesis since middle school was also in the class. Eve told me how she and Cole fought a lot before the university, and there were times I wanted to confront Cole, but Eve never allowed it. Eve told me from day one never to fight her battles for her, especially with Cole. I respected that.

In the classroom, Cole acted like a little girl every time Eve participated, making snarky remarks. I allowed the behavior until midterms. I just could not watch from the sidelines anymore. For midterms, our professor assigned each group a topic and said each person had to write an essay, and then there would be debates between groups about the topics. Eve, who was assigned leader of a pro-life group, was scheduled to go against Cole's pro-choice group. Knowing how religious Eve was and how personal the topic of abortion was to her, I gave her a pep talk minutes before the debate.

"Don't let Cole get under your skin. Remember this is just for a grade. It means nothing to you," I told Eve in our shared apartment the night before the debate and then gave her a good luck kiss.

"So, yeah, that's why abortion is not good," Eve concluded as she finished her argument in the debate and added, as she walked back to her seat, "That, plus it's wrong in God's eyes."

"This ain't church boo," Cole replied before rolling his eyes.

"Clearly. The Bible condemns abortion," Eve said, and everyone focused on her instead of the next two groups waiting at their podiums, ready to debate over rumors that a man named the Operator was really God in a human form and came down to deliver the lucky few from cruelty.

"Bitch, bye. First Corinthians 7:8–9 talks about the wrongs of premarital sex, and here you are with a baby in your belly before a wedding ring is put on your finger. Stop trying to act like a saint," Cole said.

I felt angry, but what made it worse was watching the whole class laugh. I just could not keep it in anymore. "The Bible also condemns homosexuality for those unaware. Like giving another guy a blow job in the back of a car, outside where I work," I joined in. I made it obvious whom I was hinting at by looking directly at Cole. The professor who stood in one place and observed the whole thing finally reacted. He gave me a dirty look. The whole class turned and began to laugh at Cole.

"The Bible condemns cheating, too, you perv," Cole said and made a dramatic exit. The cheating comment he made created rocky edges in my relationship with Eve. Two semesters later, Eve called me at work, crying and telling me she could not do it anymore.

"I have given you too many chances, Kurk. I am done," Eve cried. I arrived home after work, and everything with Eve's name on it was gone. The one thing Eve did not take with her was a cassette. I watched the cassette. Cole Reed had made a secret sex tape of me and one of my coworkers. Cole Reed cost me the opportunity to watch my baby boy grow up. I called everyone I knew might've had a clue about Eve's whereabouts and reached a dead-end every time, but I did not quit my search. One night, as I drove home from work during a storm, I looked out the window and saw a young lady carrying a clear rectangular box. She was soaked. She was in a rush; I assumed it was to get to a safe place, and so I offered her a ride. When she got in the car, I had a closer look at what was inside the box; it was a live serpent.

An hour passed, and there I was, lying naked next to her, back at my place. Sometimes I just couldn't help myself around beautiful women, especially younger ones.

"So what's the deal with the snake?" I finally asked her as she dressed up.

"I was on my way to do something with it before the storm hit. I have cancer. My grandmother used to tell me stories about a time when she had stage four cancer and a miracle saved her. She called it *Tales of the Fifth Night*. Apparently if you go to a deserted crossroads on the fifth day of any month and kill a serpent, then you get a wish, anything you want," she said. I did not know what to say to her.

That's just sad, I thought and smiled.

"Do you believe in the impossible, Kurk?"

"I am sorry. I am a man of science," I told her. She grabbed the box with the serpent inside from the chair I'd put it on and turned the doorknob to leave.

"That's too bad," she said.

The storm stopped, and she was gone, but what she told me about the fifth night ate away at me like a parasite until I gave in to trying it out. *What's the worst that can happen*? I thought.

On the fifth day of June, almost a whole month after my encounter with the beautiful young girl, I killed the last of five serpents on a nearby crossroads.

"I am the demigod Adameous Orionis," a man dressed in a blue suit told me. "I am a mind reader, and in all my years of deal making, I have never met anyone as unique as you, sir Kurk Benson. You correlated the number of nights with serpents and hoped to get five wishes instead of one. I see you don't only cheat ladies. I should not do this, but because of the uniqueness of your logic, I'll grant you five wishes." He made the dead serpents vanish with a snap of his fingers.

"Prick your finger here and get your wishes," the handsome yet mysterious entity suggested before he displayed a small ball with three needles instead of one. Before proceeding, I remembered a famous saying, one that says every magical deal has a price. I looked Adameous in his eyes and demanded he tell me what I had to give up for the wishes.

"Stop searching for your ex-fiancée and baby boy," he told me. It felt painful, the choice. I took a minute to think of my best option, and then I made a choice.

"Deal. Tell me what each needle means before I prick my finger," I told him. *I am not a fool*, I thought. I knew he'd heard it if he really had the ability to read minds, but I did not care.

"You really are a rare breed, Mr. Benson. Two of these needles are there to work against you. You can use one of your five wishes to know the name of two. That'll help you decide," Adameous advised.

Like every businessman I'd ever met, Adameous had an art for trickery, and he knew I was aware of it. *Deal*, I thought.

"Tall needle is called Punishment, and the short needle is called Trickery," Adameous told me.

I laughed before I pricked my finger on the middle needle.

"Wish one, while I can't look for my baby boy, I wish for him to look for me and find me one day.

"Wish two, I want my baby boy to get whatever he desires most in life when he knows what that is.

"Wish three, I wish for Cole Reed to never get a sexual sensation for the remainder of his life.

"Wish four, I wish to never be caught cheating ever again, no matter who I am with."

Sixteen years after my encounter with Adameous, I was living my dreams. Every night when my wife, Kathy, was at work, I brought a new beautiful girl to the house and had fun. If they weren't my chemistry students from the high school I taught at, they were strippers or girls I met at the clubs. A guy only lives once. One afternoon, my class was interrupted by Shaylie. Shaylie was not in my class personally, but I asked about her and heard she was a transfer student from Columbus, Georgia. I knew all the beautiful students at the school, and I was ready to bet my life that none were at Shaylie's level. *Pretty Shaylie with the round butt*, I thought every time I walked by her at the school. One afternoon, I stumbled on two guys from the basketball team discussing Shaylie. One of them, I assumed was her boyfriend, was bragging about naked pictures she'd sent him before I grabbed the phone from his hand and told him he'd need to have a private session with me if he wanted it back. I even told him if he did not prefer that option, then I would take it to the principal and ruin his basketball future. The threat worked, but before the session, I sent the photos to my phone number and then deleted all conversations.

"I did you the favor of deleting your conversations with Shaylie. Don't make this mistake again," I told him after a long stupid pep talk about morals, and then I gave him the phone back. When Shaylie visited me during my lunch break to deliver important papers from the office, I asked her for a second of her time.

"I am sure you'd hate to see them get leaked," I told Shaylie, as she stared at my phone screen. Yes. I admit I took things too far after Shaylie's arrival, but in my defense, her outfits were too revealing, and she was too beautiful. It was Shaylie's fault. Shaylie agreed to compromise. I told her what I wanted, and she agreed to it.

After cheerleading practice, Shaylie came by the house. Shaylie and I sat by my pool for a few minutes before I showed her where my wife and I slept. *Best sex I've ever had*, I thought, after intense and yet magical hours with Shaylie. I looked into Shaylie's eyes, for what I realized was the real first time because before then, I'd focused on her beautiful face and sexy body. Something about Shaylie felt strangely familiar.

"So what made you leave Georgia?" I asked Shaylie, as I continued to admire her eyes.

"As a man of science, you probably won't believe it. I was actually born a guy, and for a long time, I knew I was trapped inside the wrong body. I was miserable. All I ever wanted was to be a full girl, and one morning I woke up one. Neither me nor my mother knew how we'd explain it to the people we knew there, and so she suggested moving back here," Shaylie explained. There was a sudden pain in my heart, one I never felt before.

"What is your mother's name?" I forced myself to ask.

"Eve," Shaylie said, and it tore a hole through the ventricles of my heart.

I felt the only way to go from there was under. I held a pistol to my head the next afternoon, and before I pulled the trigger, my phone rang, and it was an unrecognizable number. He told me his name was the Operator and that he had a place where all my regrets would disappear. I followed his directions, and they led me to the infamous Tri-Rail F, a place I thought only existed in dreams. A magical tri-rail with four magical trains that journey to graceful destinations and relieve one of any tragedy.

When train number two finally arrived and the stranger and I stepped off, we came to learn Destination Two was a million times worse than any tragedy we faced back on earth.

15

Tales of Three Sisters

"The day the fifth child of a mother destined by fate to have no children bore three cousin-siblings will mark the beginning of the reckoning; the collapsing days of Destination Two."

Anivens Fazil remembered the demigod Adameous Orionis and the day he told him of this prophecy. The prophecy made no sense to Anivens until he became part of it.

Anivens remembered Adameous well. Anivens was ten years old when his father took him to a crossroad to murder him in front of Adameous. Instead of dying, Anivens watched as Adameous murdered his father in front of him.

Years later, almost a full life later, Anivens was driving on an empty road to Jersey to watch his sister, Aisha, perform live and ended up reuniting with Adameous. Anivens remembered his car flipping upside down in an attempt to avoid hitting Adameous whose appearance was sudden. Doing this sent Anivens straight into a coma, and when he came to, the most handsome individual he ever laid eyes on was standing before him in a cabin all the way in Michigan.

"I will make three bodies for you, but they'll share one mind. You will meet, love, and bed the Malik sisters. You will create a child with each, and then you'll kill one while the other two watch," Adameous demanded.

His voice was so smooth it almost persuaded Anivens not to question his cruel demands. "What if I don't want to?" Anivens asked, fighting the convincing, smooth voice that was Adameous's.

"I am the man who gave life to you and your four siblings. I linked all their lives to yours, and if I were to kill you, then their lives would fall apart, and they'd follow you to the grave."

Anivens could not force himself to believe what was unfolding in front of him, mostly because what Adameous said about his siblings scared him. *What if he's telling the truth?* Anivens thought.

Later that afternoon, though it felt scary just to wonder, Anivens asked Adameous why it was so important for him to bring about the end of this Destination Two he'd spoken of so long ago. Anivens was no stranger to the stories about the man named the Operator and his trains and their destinations. His curiosity about the link between the Operator and Adameous was too heavy, he had to ask.

"The Operator is my uncle, and because of him, my father is trapped in Destination Two. Accomplishing the prophecies of this book is the way my brother and I plan on destroying the gate of Destination Two," Adameous told him before flashing a book in front of him. The book looked more ancient than the Bible itself.

From the little he knew about Adameous, Anivens wondered if freeing the man who brought Adameous to existence was worth it.

Is my family so important? Anivens wondered before he found his single mind inside three different bodies in different corners of the world. The first body, the original, stayed the same. The second body looked a bit similar to that of Channing Tatum, except he was light-skinned. Anivens was convinced that was actually whom Adameous based the second body upon, with little exceptions. As for the third body, Anivens imagined dark-skinned Shawn Mendes with the head of Micheal Bakari Jordan. Anivens saw Adameous as a copycat with a revengeful heart but with powers he could never go against, unexplainable ones.

Fast-forward five years since their second encounter. Adameous lived up to the promise he made to Anivens after splitting his mind into three bodies and sending him after the Malik sisters.

In a crossroads, in Clarksdale, Mississippi, the sound of thunder raged over Anivens's terrified headlike lions in a cage with vipers. When the rain started, Anivens's tears rolled down his face until they reached the ground where the three Malik sisters were forced onto their knees. Adameous stood behind the sisters and made sure his invisible force field stayed intact. "You can kill yourself along with all your siblings or the ravishing Kacey Malik, the discerning Sandy Malik, or the compassionate Joe Malik," Adameous instructed.

This must have been how my father felt when he had to decide which of us to sacrifice to keep the others alive, Anivens thought in his original body and remembered his four siblings. He wondered which choice they'd want him to make. His sister Aida would've definitely chosen to live, so would his brother Ajmal. Aisha and Akeem probably would've made the selfless choice. *Guess I am the deciding factor*, Anivens thought. *I will decide if we're selfish or selfless.*

"So far it's been selfish," Adameous interrupted, reminding Anivens he had the ability to read minds.

First Anivens stared into Kacey's beautiful hazel eyes. Anivens remembered when he first felt his heart attempting to jump out of his chest for her. It was when he took her to the beautiful beach in the Bahamas. She was a poet and wrote him the most beautiful poem about a second life that exists after death, exclusively for people who discovered the last level of love for each other. "Like us," she told him after she explained. "We'll stare at beautiful mermaids who will sing the entire story of our love. Our two hearts will create a mind of their own, and as we watch, they'll try to connect like magnets." Kacey was not like any girl Anivens ever met. She was a hopeless romantic who understood him and treated him like a century-old poem she wouldn't let even a microorganism approach.

Then there was Kacey's older sister, Sandy. Anivens did not know anyone who possessed as much intellectual skill as she. But despite her smarts and her ability to find reasonable solutions to every problem they faced together, what Anivens loved most about Sandy was how she used her brain. Sandy used her smarts for the good of the unfortunate. With Sandy, Anivens was not visiting beautiful sites as he had with Kacey, but he received the same joys. Sandy engaged in many travels, helping people in third-world countries who were in need, and she tagged Anivens along on all her projects.

"You're always helping people. When will you rest?" Anivens remembered asking Sandy in a tent somewhere in Port Au Prince, Haiti, outside a boot camp Sandy helped build for young kids who could not afford an education.

"I believe I was blessed, so therefore until that blessing is gone. When I die," she replied. For a second it almost seemed like her blonde hair had glowed, as if the angels that sent her stood a bit too close and the light from their wings had reflected on her hair.

Lastly, Anivens looked at Joe, the youngest of the three. Joe was not Kacey or Sandy, not a beautiful hopeless romantic with dreams of paradise, or a genius with a genuine dream of saving everyone who was unable. With her dirty short blonde hair, and those serious dark-brown eyes that she inherited from her father, Joe was never afraid to look into your soul and tell you what you needed. Not what you wanted. She was not mean and did not have bad intentions, but Joe was a walking and talking wake-up call. "Why bother complaining to us about what your doctor says about your cholesterol problems if you'll just keep eating the same shit over and over again?" Joe asked their friend and neighbor Melisa Hinges, on a double date, during Christmas Eve the year before their marriage. "You're wasting the doc's time, your time, and our time," she finished. Of course, Melisa never asked them to double date after that, but after a few months, she started going to the gym and dieting.

"Why are you the way you are? Sometimes a little sugarcoating is good to have in life," Anivens told Joe once and regretted it immediately, mostly because of her response.

"Think of people as a piece of muscle and sugarcoating as a foam roller. When you break down muscle and let it heal on its own, it rebuilds and becomes stronger. When you just foam roll it all the time, the smallest piece of material can damage it permanently." Joe had a crooked smile on her face after she said this.

Anivens always wondered how long it had taken her to rebuild after whoever had broken her to become so strong.

After a final look at Adameous, at the three sisters, and then at the knife on his hand, the same one Adameous used to murder his father, Anivens made his choice. *Rest*, he thought.

"Kill," Anivens began.

16

Tales of Whites

More funerals. Death will never stop following me, Jesse Ortiz thought before he followed the crowd across the street.

"I knew I'd be back here in Georgia, but I always thought it would be under better circumstances," Alfonzo Ramos, Jesse's crippled best friend and roommate, said. There was something about Mountain View Baptist Church and Cemetery that intrigued Alfonzo. It was not because the church and cemetery were separated by only a road. *Was it because the cemetery has more trees than tombstones?* Alfonzo wondered. *A place made for the dead that holds so much life.* "Help me," Alfonzo demanded.

Jesse helped Alfonzo get up from the wheelchair and helped him get a feel of the green grass.

This is nature at its best, Alfonzo thought and remembered Florida, how almost the entire state was made of artificial grass. "It feels like the first time," Alfonzo told Jesse, who then smiled for the first time ever since their arrival in Georgia. Alfonzo was grateful for having a friend like Jesse, but at times, he felt guilty. Alfonzo lost loved ones, but none of the hardship he endured compared to Jesse's, and yet Jesse always went out of his way to take care of Alfonzo and his needs. *Seven funerals in two weeks was awful,* Alfonzo thought with one look at Jesse, as he too, dropped his rose over the last twin caskets to reach the surface of the cemetery ground.

Alfonzo had to forget about his own regrets when Jesse received news of the passing of the Whites. The corpses of Jesse's father, Douglass White, with his wife, Leslie; daughter, Riley; nephews, Peyton and Sky; son, Radian Rae; and daughter, Don Rae were discovered in their big mansion. The cause of the fire that burned the Whites remained a mystery.

"They were great people. They raised me like one of theirs," Alfonzo remembered Jesse crying in disbelief before Alfonzo provided him with a shoulder to cry on.

After the funeral, Jesse said his goodbyes to the friends of the family he was familiar with and drove back to the apartment he and Alfonzo stayed in. "This letter. When I showed it to the police, they made it seem like I was crazy and then said that someone was just pulling a childish prank on me. But to me, this writer seems to know too much about the Whites for him or her not to actually be the person behind the fire," Jesse said after preparing two ham-and-cheese sandwiches. He handed Alfonzo the letter, which was stained from the sriracha sauce Jesse and Alfonzo loved on their ham-and-cheese sandwiches.

"Where did you get this?" Alfonzo asked, as Jesse sat the sandwiches down in front of the television, on the coffee table.

"I found it in the mail a few days after I found out about the Whites' death," Jesse replied and sat down next to Alfonzo, so close he could smell the Old Spice deodorant Alfonzo had put on for the funeral. "The handwriting is unique—a White's. I have a gut feeling that one of our 'dead' Whites committed this crime. Everything in here is stuff we all knew and some none of us knew."

And you wonder why the police thought you were crazy? Alfonzo thought.

"How could it be a White when eight corpses were discovered?" Alfonzo asked.

"I don't know. The letter was written after their death. The handwriting seems too familiar. The writer knew so many personal things about the Whites. I'm in a maze here," Jesse said. Jesse begged Alfonzo to read the letter but not before giving him a brief overview of the eight potential suspects.

Alfonzo opened the letter and began to read as carefully as he could.

DEAR JESSE,

If you are reading this, then you heard about the passing of the Whites. Jesse, don't take that bull story from the police. The fire was not accidental. It was I who killed our family, out of mercy. All those holiday events, all those fake smiles, and fake happy moments with you during visits, I had to put an end to them. My family was a bunch of frauds, abominations I just could not force myself to share a world with anymore. First, Douglass. You have to agree the prideful bastard deserved to die. After cheating on her, the heartless pig had the audacity to leave your mom and marry Leslie. He was "always right" no matter how much he was hurting everyone around him. The fire was the second death. I killed them all individually first, right after I drugged them. With Douglass, I poisoned the bastard. He really should not have drunk that glass of milk. Now the world has one less prideful asshole to deal with. Then there was Leslie. That spoiled brat was the definition of what's wrong with modern women. She was entitled, greedy, selfish. I'll stop there because the list is just too long. Whenever it came time for your visits, she always attempted to not let it happen, and when you did come, she put on that fake face and pretended to love you like one of her own kids. That sledgehammer you and Douglass used that one summer to do work in the backyard? I made sure Leslie tasted it. I took five good swings and felt all of that bottled-up hatred for her fly out of me like rain from dark clouds. Peyton, my third kill. That fat ass just had to go. Peyton would have eaten the world if she was allowed. She just could never stop eating. I buy a cake, she wants some. I buy candies, she wants some. Ironically, I poisoned her, too, but instead of using a beverage like I did her Uncle Douglass, I made Peyton a cheesecake. The saying is right, "What you love most is what will get you killed." Fourth one to go was Riley. In my entire life, I have never met a lazier individual. Do you know how many times I asked Riley for a favor, an important favor, and she turned me down, to do something as stupid as binge-watching shows on Netflix. *Riley wanted to take the whole "*Netflix *and chill" thing to the next level, so I helped her out. I used the couch foam that she "sooo adored" and gave her a permanent chill.*

My fifth kill was Sky. She was just a horrible human being. For someone who lived with an uncle, I expected Sky to know her place, but that did not happen. Sky was always fighting at school and being suspended for it. She had serious anger issues and her uncle Douglass never disciplined her, and so I did it for him. I used one of Douglass's belts and choked Sky with it. Now that's punishment. For number sixth, the prince of the Whites, Holden, I saved the crown jewel. Ever since he was little, the greedy bastard never had enough. If Holden was not fighting for more parental time, he was fighting to have the better outfits. Do you know how hurtful it was to watch greedy old Holden get, get, get, and get while Douglass and Leslie gave the rest of the family minimum? I gave, gave, gave, and gave Holden a taste of their sharpest knife, right in his chest. And lastly, the twins, Don Rae, and Radian Rae. I never met anyone who gave meaning to the term hater *more than Don Rae. I learned Don Rae sabotaged my best friend's three-year relationship, all because she could not stand the fact that she was not dating the hottest guy in our grade. Don Rae even screwed Melina Orbin from cheerleader tryouts, all because she knew Melina was better and would've won head cheerleader. That jealous scumbag had this coming to her for years. I laugh even as I write this because remembering what was left of her pretty face after I forced it on that hot stove is just too hilarious. Radian Rae was my favorite, and that is why I saved him for last. Radian was a new breed of abomination. I think the only thing his mind ever processed was sex. I never told anyone this, but at one time, Radian sexually abused me. It didn't matter that our last names were the same, as long as he took the urges off. Radian brought a different girl into our home almost every freaking night. It was disrespectful, not because I was in the same house or that he had a great girlfriend, but because a lot of the girls were too drunk to even know their own names. I cut Radian's penis into a million pieces and watched him bleed to death. So, Jesse, don't waste your time tearing over my family.*

When he finished, Alfonzo gave the letter back to Jesse. "I disagree with cops. I think this killer pre-planned the whole thing, including when the letter would get to you. I'm sorry. Try not to stress over it. A coward will stay a coward."

Jesse smiled and set the letter aside. Jesse and Alfonzo began to eat the ham-and-cheese sandwiches. Deep down, Alfonzo knew the identity of the true killer lay in between the lines of the letter. Could Leslie White, who he assumed was the killer have written the letter, committed the murders, and then committed suicide in the fire, or could it have been someone else who knew the Whites too well, Alfonzo wondered.

17

Dark Destination Tale

I am stuck. I always told my sister, Anne, that a story told for too long will eventually shift. A story told by more than one person and heard by many stops being a fact and becomes fiction. It becomes a rumor.

One famous rumor Anne and I heard growing up was of a mystical being named the Operator. It was said he came to earth and built four magical trains tasked with delivering the lucky to destinations of wonders, freedom, magic, and everything else we could possibly dream of. I am now learning not all four of those trains really deliver us from the evil grip of earth. I've come to the conclusion that the Operator may not be who history says he is. He uses deception and manipulation to get his way. I am a living example.

When I arrived at the tri-rail, I never expected my destination, Destination Four, to be a dark one. Here, I am surrounded by endless darkness; it feels as if I am trapped in a nightmare. My eyes were removed from their sockets. I can feel the presence of my brain, my heart, and my nose, but there was no anatomical linkage. I am beginning to feel as though these three organs are just suspended in midair, in whatever this dark place is. As of now, I think I will be stuck here for eternity. I can't help but wonder, though, why I can still smell, and why the only things I can smell are tree roots, soil, and decaying bones. I do not deserve to spend eternity here.

Three things led me here—a misconception of the Operator's motive, my personal belief, and Marvin Keys. These three things, believe it or not, correlate, as if fate were adding fruit to the salad bowl that was my life.

"You don't believe in the Operator?" Anne asked me.

My therapist, Jackie Bernes, repeated this same question during one of our sessions.

"No, I don't. I don't believe in 'God' and you think I'd believe in some impostor trying to be him?" I said right before chuckling. This was my response to both of them.

"I hear each train is based upon humans' way of life, our beliefs," Jackie said. I wished she were more like Anne, who did her best to never argue with me, even when it was friendly arguments. Of course, I understood Jackie was being paid to somewhat argue.

"I don't believe in anything," I told her, and I could tell it frustrated her. Sometimes I wondered if she ever thought of just standing up and walking out on one of our sessions.

"Not believing in anything, believe it or not, is a belief on its own," she finished that afternoon. I remember till this day. Here I am now, learning how right Jackie was all along. I should have believed in something.

I was not always a nonbeliever. I lost my belief on the same day I lost my virginity. The day I was raped.

I was seventeen years old, in high school. My best friend at the time, Cassie Wobbler, heard about what was rumored to be the biggest Halloween party of the year. *College chicks only*, it said on the flyer in bold.

"You seriously think we'll be the only high schoolers there pretending to be college girls?" Cassie asked, and when I nodded, she rolled her eyes and continued to do my makeup.

"Please cut yourself some slack and enjoy this. You have a 4.5 GPA, so you deserve this," she added. Little did we know, we were going there to be drugged by some balloon heads from out of town who posed as in-state college guys. Their gray eye contacts, dark angel wings, and white feather masks should have warned us to run but instead pulled us in.

Cassie was no stranger to sex, and so I was certain she was not feeling the pain I was enduring as two of the six guys simultaneously penetrated my vaginal canal, introducing it to new sensations, hellish ones. By the time the sixth of them passed through, Cassie's and then my hymen had become nonexistent. My blood and tears, which soaked their bedsheets, was evidence of that.

In the midst of all that pain, I prayed for my entire soul out to anything or anyone who was listening, to rescue me, but nothing happened. I, the Christian girl who strongly believed in sex after marriage and that God and Christ had my back always, no longer believed in fairy tales.

The worst part was that the guys got away with it. When the cops questioned us, all Cassie and I could remember were the tattoos of the bloomed roses surrounding a vagina. They all had it on their biceps. Sadly, it did no good in helping the cops. Cassie committed suicide a year later, and I ended up in therapy. From the age of seventeen to twenty-seven, I never looked at a guy romantically or sexually the same.

When I turned twenty-eight, my sister Anne was invited to a ball by her boss, John K. Corbin, CEO of John's Design, a multimillion-dollar company that specialized in everything fashion-related. I attended the ball because Anne begged, but when he walked in, I knew that if I had not come, it would have been my loss. I knew I had to put down all of my barriers for a chance to dance under the luminary stars that were his eyes. *They must have been responsible for the earth's gravitational pull*, I thought as the invisible force pushed me to move closer to where he stood by himself, with a brandy glass in hand.

As I approached him, maybe it was the three champagne glasses I'd had, but every inanimate object in the room screamed, "Mistake, turn back and run!"

I should have listened, but it's like I was his Pinocchio that night. I made myself visible to him. I stood under the glimmering lights and removed my black-and-gold satin ribbon tie mask. Christina Perri's second version of "A Thousand Years" was playing, and he approached me, at the same moment Steve Kazee joined in.

"A dance?" he asked.

I ignored the familiarity in his voice but gave him my hand. He led me to the middle of the dance floor, and under those almond-shaped, galaxy designed, heterochromia eyes of his (one hazel and the other amber), it felt like a magical dance destined to last a thousand years. I was not Cinderella, and he was not a prince. When the clock touched twelve, I did not run. I was too frozen by an invisible force. I was unable to move until he asked for my number, and I gave it, despite the inanimate objects' objection. Marvin Keys turned out to be his name, and as the song goes, after our first date, when he took me to Paris, *"All of my doubts went away and I knew that I found a home for my heart."* And then our thousand years had come to an end.

After Marvin proposed, we decided to move in together. Marvin spoke of passed demons a lot but never went into details, but one day, I came face-to-face with one. One box was too heavy. I dropped it, and after Marvin rushed over to help me clean up my mess, he picked up something that grabbed my attention. It was an old photo of a bunch of young guys. "What was this about?" I asked Marvin later that night, showing him the photo.

Marvin shrugged and said, "A very dark time of my life. Those five guys and I were best friends in college. We did some regretful things together. That night was the worst."

"Why was it?" I asked and fought not to scream.

"They took things too far. We wore stupid temporary tattoos, Halloween masks, and…"

Marvin began to cry. I threw the photo aside and went to him. I ended his pain. In one hand I held the photo and in the other a knife. Marvin did not know that until I stabbed him with it. I sent the point of the knife on a journey for his spleen. In the middle of panicking, I pulled the knife out and aimed it at my throat, but before I did anything, I received a call.

"Wrong was done to you," the Operator said after introducing himself. "Cops won't care if he and his buddies raped you as a girl. Follow these instructions, and come to me. One of my trains will take you to where you deserve to go."

As the Operator gave the instructions, I changed out of my bloody clothes.

And now here I am, where train number four dropped me off—an endless nightmare rich in soil.

18

Tales of Memory Lost

Dallas Beckman sat under the blue mango tree and observed closely. First a little girl with golden hair, longer than her arms, flew above him on the most beautiful pony he'd seen since his arrival, tossing down daisies, putting smiles on the faces of everyone around. Then butterflies with chameleon abilities flew by and blessed them with a rainbow-like performance. As they changed the colors and designs of their wings, glitter poured down like rain. Lastly, everyone in the vast garden, except him, stood up and began to sing along with a flock of mockingbirds.

Dallas admitted to himself, all of the wonders of this new home were, as rumored, perfect. But Dallas was far from joyful. "Where the trains will take you is full of magic and beautification. Sadness does not exist there," Dallas remembered overhearing his coworker Travis tell their manager, Nancy.

Of course, Dallas never trusted the idea of magical trains on earth because Dallas was a Jehovah's Witness, and to him, it sounded like Satan's trickery. To his surprise, Dallas found everything about the place as promised and worth living for, but no matter how hard Dallas tried, he could not be as joyful as everyone else. Dallas knew why. Deep inside, Dallas knew that sadness lay behind a wall in his mind. *What am I supposed to remember?* Dallas wondered in frustration, under the same blue mango tree, every day since his arrival, right before he cried in secrecy.

"I'm miserable and I can't seem to remember why. I feel a blank canvas in my head. Were some of my memories erased?" Dallas asked the Operator's proxy as he was caught crying alone one night.

"Yes. The Operator did not want me to let you feel a burden too heavy. Whatever it was he made me take from you was for your own benefit," the old man with silver long hair replied. But it didn't bring Dallas the comfort he wanted, a comfort Dallas had admitted in defeat he'd lived for eternity without.

It all began years earlier, with a love affair. Dallas' wife, Krista, knocked on a stranger's door and received no response. "If they don't open up, then check under the wrecked car that's in the driveway. There's usually a spare key there." Krista remembered the suited handsome man who tipped her off. She followed his instructions, and it led her to the bedroom where she discovered her husband, Dallas, in bed with another man, his childhood friend, officer John K. Corbin. Things heated among the three. John, who knew nothing of Krista's existence, also felt betrayed.

"Pack your things as soon as you get home. You're supposed to be a Jehovah's Witness, and here you are committing the biggest sin alive!" Krista said before she slammed the door.

"All this time I kept saying I've never been happier with anyone. It was all a show. I don't want to be part of your double life. Walk out and never come back," John told Dallas.

From that day, Dallas's life fell apart, but the love he had for both Krista and John would not go away. Not being next to either of them at night nearly drove him mad, made him desperate. So Dallas did what he considered a last resort: he went to his coworker Travis for stories. Travis told Dallas many stories, but only one stood out to him—one about the fifth night of any month. Dallas found a deserted crossroad on the fifth night of the next month and murdered a live serpent, as the story instructed. Dallas expected disappointment, but a man dressed in a suit appeared before him. "Do you honestly believe it is possible for one person to be equally in love with two people, Mr. Beckman?" the man asked, and Dallas almost turned and ran. *This is the devil*, Dallas thought. *How could I be betraying Jehovah like this?*

"There's a middle ground to all things," Dallas replied.

"Maybe, but eventually our instincts lead us to one side and not the other, but that's not why you're here. Make your wish. You did everything as told."

"I wish for a way to have both Krista and John without ever having to choose," Dallas forced himself to say. After he said this, the man in the suit pulled out a small ball with three needles and asked him to prick his finger.

"What's the price?" Dallas asked as he pricked his finger on one of the needles.

"You already paid for it. For your wish to be true, convince Krista you changed, and she'll take you back. As for John, I will create a person and implement him in history like he was already there, but it will be your mind guiding him. You'll have two bodies and one mind. However, remember when the end comes, they will take one road."

Before Dallas could ask the man what it all meant, the man was gone. As for Dallas, he found Krista again two months later as the man predicted. She did take him in. After his reunion with Krista, Dallas felt what the man had said would happen; his mind had divided. He couldn't explain it, but he was living as two people with two different bodies. The body created for John was a bit taller and looked like actor Theo James, except he had blond hair and blue eyes. He was given the name Eddie Burbaker. As the man in the suit promised Dallas, Eddie was placed in the same police force as officer John K. Corbin. It did not take Eddie long to make John fall in love with him. Dallas wondered if this was due to the wish or because he was the one inside Eddie's head.

As himself, Dallas could not imagine a better life with Krista, the wonderful woman whom he had rescued from an abusive relationship and fallen in love with.

As Eddie, he could not imagine a happier life with officer John. His double life went well for two years, and then it all came down to one road as the man in the suit had warned.

Heading east on Sydney Harbour Bridge, Dallas received an alarming call. It was his wife, Krista.

"Baby," she said. There was a terror to her breaking voice. Dallas sensed her fear. "He's here. Santino is here, and he has a gun. He's in our home. Please hurry," she whispered, withholding tears. Santino Albezius was Krista's abusive ex-husband whom Dallas had helped her leave. He was also mentally unstable. That was why Dallas had taken Krista and moved to another state.

"Don't do anything to provoke him. I'm coming!" Dallas told Krista. Dallas sounded his horn, hoping the cars in front would let him pass.

"Baby, I am scared," Krista finished right before her screams almost burst Dallas's eardrums. At the sound of Santino's angry voice in the background, Dallas's instinct took over, forcing him to make a U-turn.

What Dallas did not know was that Krista had called the police before calling him. Heading west, there he was, officer Eddie Burbaker heading to the house at lightning speed. When Dallas made the U-turn, the collision sent the police car off the bridge and down to the water below and landed Dallas's Hyundai just a few feet away from the newly broken barrier. Dallas's two bodies. His original and Eddie had never been this close to each other before. Dallas watched in terror from above the bridge where he was stuck in his car as Eddie fought to open the doors to escape. Water began to fill the car. *What happens if I die as Eddie?* Dallas wondered for the very first time since his wish was made. After hearing through his police radio that officer John K. Corbin had arrived at Krista's house a minute too late, Eddie fought harder to not drown.

Shaky, Dallas forced himself out of the wrecked car and rushed to Eddie's rescue. He dove head-first, as the people stood there and watched, some calling emergency units, and others too busy recording to care. The fall was tough. Reaching the car, Dallas pulled on the door from the outside, and when it was not opening, Dallas thought of breaking the window; and before he could, he felt his conscious mind jump from his body. As Eddie, Dallas watched as his original body, with no life in it, went under. Eddie fought his hardest to open the door from the inside until water filled up the car, then his lungs. Dallas, trapped inside Eddie's body, then fell unconscious.

Am I dead? Dallas wondered. He was no longer in the water, and his mind was back into his original body. He was wrapped in seagrass, his clothes were soaked, and he was clueless as to what happened after he fell unconscious.

He laid eyes on the ocean water and spotted her. She swam closer toward the shore until her red mermaid tails, which matched her long curly hair, transformed into human legs.

"You are in Ellesmere Island. He heard you were in trouble and sent me to rescue you. Now you must go the rest of the journey to him on your own," she said in her angelic voice.

"Where must—" Dallas began.

"Go straight for three miles, close your eyes, and think of Krista," she instructed before she ran back and jumped into the water, her tail disappearing before his very eyes. He turned away from the water and did as she instructed. When he opened his eyes again, there he was, in a long hallway made entirely out of white marble. There were four doors in a hall that seemed as if it had no end.

"What is this place?" Dallas asked and hoped someone was indeed listening. Before he spotted a man standing a few feet away, Dallas looked at the ceiling and saw them, floating dream catchers, each displaying a different time of his life, like videos on replay. *Is this the afterlife?* Dallas wondered. The silver-haired old man dressed in old-time clothes moved closer.

"Welcome, Dallas Beckman, to what many know as Destination Three. You didn't get here by train. How'd you get here?" the old man asked, and it confused Dallas.

What train could he be referring to? Dallas wondered before he told the old man about the redheaded mermaid who informed him of the strange place. "How do I get out of here?" Dallas asked and finally realized where he might have been.

"You have to pass the Operator's test first," the man replied, and it confirmed what Dallas guessed was happening. Dallas knew he was at one of those destinations Travis always talked about.

"What's the test?" Dallas asked. *If this part of the story is true, then my wife Krista and John could be given back to me*, Dallas thought, *and I actually didn't die*. With one look at them, all the floating dream catchers came down and surrounded the two of them until they had taken up the whole hallway.

"There are two million memories here, and they're all of you. Thanks to the Operator, you will remember them all as if they happened yesterday, simultaneously. Out of them all, there are two that define your entire life. You'll pick the ones you think they are, and you'll have the ability to alter them. Based on how you alter the memories, you'll be sent to either Destination One where Krista will be waiting for you, or Destination two," the man said.

Dallas looked at the memories again. There was no way that was possible. "Why do I have to do all that? Can't the Operator just let me through? That's what he does, right?" Dallas asked.

"Well, he has rules about his destinations, and though you were almost perfect enough for One, one stain in your life makes this test necessary."

"What if I pick the wrong memory?" Dallas asked.

"Well, the whole journey you had here will repeat itself like a loop," the man replied, without displaying any sympathy. "You probably have already had this conversation with me and do not know it. Out of every two hundred individuals that end up here, only twenty ever actually pass the test, and out of that amount, only three usually end up at Destination One afterward," the man admitted.

This brought back Dallas's anxiety. "Is John there too?" Dallas asked before he grabbed the first dream catcher.

"I can't answer that," the man said before handing him the second dream catcher. Without feeling a tiny bit of fatigue, Dallas finally reached dream catcher number three hundred and fifty. "This one. I pick this one." Dallas held on to the dream catcher tightly and waited for the ability to alter it.

In the dream catcher, Dallas was just a young boy, and he had just met John K. Corbin for the first time. *Maybe Jehovah's been the Operator all along, and behind all of it*, Dallas thought. *Maybe removing John has been the answer.* As an alteration, Dallas changed his younger self's destination, causing him to have never met John K. Corbin.

"The Operator is more than proud," the old man said. "Now be with Krista and forever forget this stain." He touched Dallas's forehead, removing every memory of Krista and of ever meeting John K. Corbin. For he knew that Krista would not be waiting for Dallas's arrival in Destination One.

19

Tearful Butterfly Tale

The love in my heart is you. Always was. Whenever I was not with you, I felt like my life meant nothing. Wherever I end up now will be hell if you're not there by my side, the words echoed in Cesar Sifuentes's head as he stared at the wall. It was like this almost every night ever since Joy Laudenslager died, one needle after the other.

"Joy, all I want is for you to always be mine and for me to always be yours, but your father has a point. Time is passing, and I want your future to be luxurious. I would never forgive myself to know that your future was not a great one because of me. This is the hardest thing to do, but we can no longer be together. Not right now at least. One day, when you're finished, and if your heart still belongs to mine, then we can find our way back to each other."

Cesar remembered Joy's eyes were soaked, but she remained speechless.

"Joy, as you can see, my life is the example of why going to that school is a priority. The last thing I want is for our kids to have to live the nightmare I am living now."

When Cesar tried to leave that night, Joy wrapped herself around his feet like an albino Burmese python and cried like a two-year-old until she fell asleep, and he escaped.

Cesar's mind took him on many journeys, most of which were of Joy, when it was under the influence of all the drugs. If this was the closest he'd ever get to her, then all the drugs were worth it, Cesar convinced himself.

Cesar never forgot when he first met Joy; he relived those early days constantly. "Excuse me, why are you crying?" one of the twins had asked Cesar back when he was a month into middle school.

"Because life sucks. No one wants to be my friend," Cesar admitted and almost burst out crying again.

With both hands on her hips, the sassy little girl replied, "Well, I'm Joy, and that's my sister, Vicky. I want to be your friend, and I'll prove it." She dug in her lunch bag until she found a Graham cracker. She gave it to him, and he happily accepted it. Their friendship lasted a long while. He escorted her to the final middle school dance when her date caught chicken pox and canceled on her. She helped him graduate by tutoring him for thirty minutes every time they hung out outside of school. When she broke curfew for the first time to attend a college party she was forbidden from attending, he lied for her. In high school, she bought him everything he needed to attend prom, even though she was not his date.

"There is a special guy who has been there for me ever since sixth grade, and tonight in front of all of you, I would like to ask him if he'd be okay with me taking him out on an official date and also be my first dance of the night," she announced to their graduating class, without looking nervous, after they announced her as the prom queen.

"Joy, I can't afford this place. Can I buy you food at McDonald's?" he asked before turning his face away in shame. She had bought him his school lunch from sixth grade to high school graduation. Some days when she did not attend school, he spent the whole day hungry and went to bed as such. She even offered to force her dad to pay for his college, but he fought her on it till she gave up. It was not easy.

"I asked you. I got the expenses as long as you keep your heart honest and fair toward others," she told him, and he promised her he would.

At twenty-one, Vicky introduced Joy to weed. "I'll like whatever you like," Cesar remembered saying when Joy offered him a blunt for the very first time. Gorilla Glue was the name of the first weed he smoked with Joy, and though they agreed on it as a favorite, it did not stop them from exploring. Blue Dream, Girl Scout Cookies, OG Kush, Sunset Sherbet, Gelato, White Widow, etc. You name it, they smoked it, but it was never without the presence of each other. One afternoon, Joy received a random call from Vicky, who could not stop bragging about something new on the market, something better than any weed or other influential substances. "I ordered a few things from him, but I won't make it in time to meet. Will you go meet him for me?" Vicky asked, and though Joy hated the idea, Cesar forced her to say yes.

"Are you Alfonzo Ramos from Florida?" Cesar asked, and the seventeen-year-old boy nodded before he looked around to make sure there were no cops around.

"Tell Vicky the Butterfly Tear is inside the purple bag and to be careful when opening it," Alfonzo instructed, with hair so curly it almost made Cesar envious.

"What's it made of?" Cesar asked.

"What's so special about it?" Joy followed.

Alfonzo pulled the two of them close like they were in an episode of *Gossip Girl* and told them. "My boss said this product is made from the blending of sea salt and the Queen Alexandra's birdwing. They say its effect is so strong it almost feels like actual magic. No other substance has that effect on the entire planet," Alfonzo told them.

To Cesar, something about the drug felt off.

"Let my baby and me try one free sample, and if you're telling the truth, I'll buy a year's worth," Joy demanded.

* * * * *

Cesar stopped reminiscing and fell asleep on the destroyed couch. The next morning, he skipped showering and breakfast and rushed to flip burgers at the Burger King he worked at. He sensed all the employees talked about him behind his back, about him stinking up the place, but he was always too dead on the inside to care. On his way home from work, he stopped for a bag of chips at the nearest gas station.

Near the cash register, two men approached, one in a wheelchair. He recognized him as Alfonzo Ramos. Of course, it had been ages since he'd seen him, and Alfonzo was not in a wheelchair when they first met. *I wondered how that happened*, Cesar thought before he spoke up. "Hi," he said, and the two gentlemen greeted him with a confused look. "Alfy, it's me, Cesar. I didn't think you'd ever come back to Georgia. Please take my number. Let me buy you lunch or something."

"I don't remember you," Alfonzo Ramos replied.

"I was with the twins. My girlfriend bought a whole year's worth of Butterfly Tear from you," Cesar told him.

That's when it all came back to Alfonzo. "I think Joy was her name," Alfonzo said unsure, and Cesar nodded his head repeatedly to confirm this. "I am only here for a few days for a funeral. I'll call you, and we can set up that lunch." Alfonzo could not help but honor the promise. Alfonzo thought it was mostly because he was curious as to what exactly happened to Joy. He remembered her well; she was cheerful most of the time he spent around her. He doubted she ever actually unlocked sad hormones or had a sad moment ever.

Alfonzo knew a drug head when he saw one. He used to sell to them, and at one point of his life, he tried a few of his products on them, and so he knew Cesar was deep into the life of a drug head. His skin was peeling off on the table, but Alfonzo remained unalarmed. He did not want to offend. And it's not like he could have gotten up and walked away; he was stuck in his wheelchair, and it was Cesar who had driven them to the cafe.

"What do you want, Cesar?" Alfonzo asked. Being blunt reminded him of his drug-selling years. That was one of the first few lessons his boss ever taught him when it came to living life as a drug dealer.

"Some of that dope stuff you sold us back then, Butterfly Tear." The desperation in those sleepless red eyes of Cesar made Alfonzo more grateful for having put that life behind him. But at the same time, Alfonzo could not help but guess Cesar must have been dealing with an overwhelming loneliness that he could relate to.

"Alfy, when I lost Joy, my entire world came crashing down. I've locked myself into everything in an attempt to feel her with me, but nothing works like I want. The Butterfly Tear will help me tremendously. It's really good," Cesar begged.

"Have you ever lost someone you cared about so much that you'd go through hell if it meant another second with her?" he asked, and tears rolled down those red eyes of his.

It pained Alfonzo to see this, mostly because it reminded him of Giovanni and how painful watching him die was. "I retired from that life a long time ago. After the Queen Alexandra's birdwing ended up on the endangered list and an investigation was done, the manufacturing of Butterfly Tear was banned a while back. There may be a guy here in Georgia who could still get you some, but I'll only tell you his name and the last address I remember if you open up to me about Joy. Tell me how she died," Alfonzo demanded. Alfonzo knew druggies; he knew it would take a thought or two, but Cesar would compromise.

"Her father came home one summer, and we had a private conversation. He basically blamed me for her not going to a big university. He said I held her back and that if I ever cared about her, then I'd break up with her and convince her to go to Oxford. She was accepted and decided on majoring in plant science. It took the last pump of my heart, but I did what was best for her," Cesar told him.

Alfonzo did not know why, but he knew it; Cesar hadn't opened up to anyone about Joy's death before him. "How'd she die?" Alfonzo asked.

It took Cesar a while to admit to Alfonzo that Joy committed suicide after two weeks at Oxford, but he did it. "Overdose," Cesar said and reached in his dirty pants pockets and pulled something out. It was a letter. Alfonzo read Joy's goodbye to Cesar, and it crushed his heart too.

"His name is Akeem Floyd. I'll text you his address," Alfonzo said. He knew he would never see or hear from Cesar again, but he knew he'd make peace with it.

Cesar contacted Akeem, and to his surprise, the number was still operational. At midnight, he met Akeem in a corner outside his house, with four times the amount he paid Alfonzo the first time he and Joy ever purchased Butterfly Tear.

Back in his messy home, Cesar sat on the couch and stared for a few minutes at a picture he'd taken of him and Joy at their high school prom. Then he opened the pill bottle of Butterfly Tear, which had come in liquid form the first time he'd had it. He took one of the pills and lost consciousness after a minute, just like the first time.

My sister said it's really like magic. I hear you'll see the last person you thought of before swallowing the syrup. Some people even reported their minds linking when they took that shit together, Joy's voice echoed as Cesar faded deeper into what he once referred to as the "forbidden land" of his mind. Then he landed.

Cesar stood up, and everything looked as it had the first time he journeyed into the Forbidden Land. The cornfield looked as if it was frozen in time and hadn't been tampered with. After reaching the end of the cornfield and reaching the astonishing waterfall hidden in the enchanted forest he'd discovered with his lover, Joy, Cesar searched around. From snakes sidewinding to birds chirping, monkeys squeaking, and the plants whistling, Cesar could not imagine any other place that compared.

"I believe it's me you're looking for, handsome devil," a soft, low voice said behind Cesar, and it startled him. There she stood in a garden of California poppies of all colors, the love of his life, in uniformity with the forest; her skirt made entirely of ferns and pink magnolias, which hung on to her breast like a magical bra. He rushed to her and lifted her off her bare feet, and like the movies, this spooked some butterflies and made them fly, mostly all around them.

"I didn't think you'd really be here," Cesar told Joy with tears of joy floating off his cheek and nourishing the shrubs in the nearby hardwood trees.

"Not for long. The owner of this place said he'd only let me wait until you came, and then I'd have to leave for the train," Joy said.

"What train?" Cesar asked. He came there a lot, and not once did he recall meeting any guy or hear about any trains.

"Well, this place has a different meaning when you're dead in the real world," Joy said.

"She's right, Cesar," someone else said, and Joy and Cesar turned to find a middle-age man, with long silver hair standing where Cesar stood before. "Joy can't stay here forever because the Operator demanded she get on her train, but if you want to come with her, then it's up to you," the man informed Cesar, and then vanished.

"Cesar, you can't. I have no idea where this train will take me," Joy said.

"Well, there's no place that could be worse than hell, and we agreed we'd go there for and with each other, so tell me what to do," Cesar said and waited for Joy to tell him what to do. When Joy finished, Cesar woke up.

Cesar admired the beautiful prom picture for one final time and then swallowed the entire bottle of Butterfly Tear. When he landed deep enough into his subconscious, Cesar found himself next to his lover again, hand-in-hand as the two waited in an empty green field before train number two (the number on both of their tickets) stopped for them to enter.

20

Tales of Spider's Web

Hell is a place. Hell is a person. Hell is an idea. Over decades, many have debated over which of these is the truth. Sit back and let me tell you a tale about my all-time favorite person, Alfonzo Ramos. After I am done, you can decide for yourself.

After being forced into a wheelchair, compliment of a bullet from his adopted, now deceased son, Giovanni Salvador, and before being taken out of the world by his own daughter, Beverly Miller, whom he did not know about until his final last breath, my magical tri-rail had the absolute honor of receiving Ramos as a guest, for what turned out to be his second-to-last visit. It began like this.

* * * * *

A week after their trip from Georgia, for the funeral of Jesse Ortiz's entire family, the Whites, Ramos woke up to a banging on his bedroom door. "Jess, is that you?" Ramos asked calmly, though deep down he knew Jesse never banged on the door that aggressively. Ramos was terrified. *Is he going to kill me too?* Ramos wondered and remembered the letter that was sent to Jesse, describing the individual deaths of his entire family, a letter in which Ramos decoded to learn that his new best friend Jesse, while he might be unaware, was the killer of the Whites.

Ramos looked around the room, and aside from the uncapped bottle of fentanyl on the floor near his bed, nothing seemed unusual, though he wished he could recall the night before. No matter how hard he tried, he just hit a blank.

"We said open up!" an angry voice screamed from behind the door, and it forced Ramos to look for his wheelchair, which was not in the room. "Walk...walk." Ramos heard the walls around him whispering. Ramos hesitated at first, but after another bang on the door, he touched the ground, and to his surprise, the wound and the pain that Giovanni's bullet had caused were gone. *I can walk*, Ramos rejoiced. *How is this possibl—*

Before Ramos finished, the door came crashing in, motivating him to jump aside, quick reflex and such.

What shocked Ramos more than the miracle of his walking that morning was the four guys who walked in. Questions floated in Ramos's head, as he studied them, in an attempt to understand what or who they were before provoking them, intentionally or not. They had the same architectural designs as human beings as far as their bodies were concerned, with the exception of the four hairy horns on each of their heads. They were white but not Caucasian. White as snow but clear enough to be mistaken for ice statues and for their diverse colored organs to be seen. They only wore pants and boots, as silver as bars of steel, probably as hard too.

"What the fuck are you things!" Ramos shouted loudly, hoping it would grab Jesse's attention, if he hadn't left for work yet. Instead, it angered the four impostors, and at the revealing of one of their blue pointy teeth, the other three held up the crystal ends of their medieval spears and aimed them at Ramos's throat.

"Soldiers, stand down!" one familiar voice screamed from outside, and Ramos felt relieved. *I am dreaming*, Ramos thought and hoped to wake up. Adamis Orionis, a man Ramos met as a little boy, in what he was told was a dream by his aunty, walked into the broken doorway.

"You're not dreaming, my dear Alfy!" Adamis said in a voice as calm as Ramos remembered. "My uncle, the Operator, has decided it's time for you to journey to one of his destinations again. He could have called you like the rest, but you've proven to be a special case and therefore he sent us to escort you."

"Tell 'Operator' I am not interested. My life has not been so great, but I'd rather take my chances here on earth. The last time I went to one of his tri-rails, I walked out with a heart that can only operate on ice!"

"My dear Alfy…we weren't asking," Adamis said and began to conjure sparks of ice on the tip of his right index finger. "My uncle has a list of special cases, and I am afraid it's your turn to go. Defy us, and Jesse will know hell here on earth. We'll begin by exposing what he did to those poor Whites."

There was something more sinister about Adamis. Ramos wondered what it was. He was no longer the gentle guy who helped lost kids find their way.

Adamis led the way, and Ramos followed, with four bodyguards behind them. Outside the house was a van. At first Ramos thought it was perfectly normal, but after he was forced inside and wings appeared on the sides to replace the tires and the van became invisible to the naked eye, Ramos tossed out the assumption.

Away from the center of Tri-Rail F, Ramos waited, alongside twelve others whom he was certain were also considered special cases. Adamis walked around and handed each of them a ticket. Unsurprisingly to Ramos, everyone had a ticket for train number two. After handing him his ticket, Adamis whispered into Ramos's ear, "Look in between the branches of that tree over there, and tell me what you see."

"A spiderweb. Why?" Ramos asked before taking a second look.

"What's strange about it?" Adamis asked, and it reminded Ramos of their first encounter. Ramos knew Adamis always had a trick up his sleeve. So he forced himself to try to figure out what Adamis wanted him to discover this time around.

"There's no spider in the web," Ramos responded.

Adamis laughed before he turned Ramos's attention back to the web and said, "The opposite."

Ramos focused more on the web until he spotted them finally. There were at least three spiders on the web. "How'd I miss that?" Ramos asked, astonished.

"Because they blend in. Those spiders are special just like you. I am not supposed to tell you this, but I want you to remember 'spot a spider in a web and you shall escape Destination Two,'" Adamis finished before the sound of the second train blasted through Ramos's ears, almost making him deaf. When the train stopped, some rushed in, and others were forced in.

Silence owned the trained until one of the guys said out loud, "I can't fucking wait to enjoy Destination Two!"

"Are you stupid?" a second one asked. "My grandma used to tell me stories about Tri-Rail F, and from her experience, Two is a prison worse than hell itself!"

Ramos recognized the voice that said this. To confirm, it was who he assumed. Ramos turned around. His eyes met hers. They said each other's names out loud.

"Jasmine," Alfonzo said.

"Alfon!" Jasmine moved to sit closer to Ramos.

"Jas, I thought you died," Ramos said and broke down in tears. Jasmine Cartaret was the only woman lucky enough to ever capture Alfonzo Ramos's frozen heart. They were only twenty years old, but they believed they had discovered every mystery there was to love. Unfortunately, Jasmine hated that Ramos was a drug dealer. He was deep into it. And when she broke the news to him that her mom was dying of cancer and her family was unable to afford treatment, he was willing to do whatever he could to help. Alfonzo and a few friends broke into the nearest local bank, and as fate would have it, the rookie policeman who first arrived on the scene that night was none other than Jasmine's father, Omar Cartaret. You can figure out what conspired from there.

"I let you think that because of everything that happened," Jasmines replied and joined in the tears. "I never stopped loving you, Alfon, but I could never imagine looking into your eyes after I found out you were part of the reason I became an orphan," Jasmine admitted, and then the train stopped moving.

"Arrivals. Please make your way out of the train, and proceed to the wondrous world that awaits you!" the speakers suggested, each with a different voice, before the same horned creatures rushed into the train and began to clear it, forcing the majority to move out.

"Jasmine, I never stopped loving you either. Destination Two is a prison, and to escape it, I want you to look for anything usual. Spot a spider in the web and you shall escape!" Ramos told Jasmine, even though he had no idea what it meant for himself. Alfonzo was forced to watch, as Jasmine was pulled away from his arms and dragged out of the train first.

21

Tales of Peaceful Waves

The story was the same, but the ending was different. On the pier, the night was cold, but it fazed them not, for their two hearts long adapted. In the beginning, they bowed to the earth and raised heads at the stars with wonder and appreciation. Compliant became their primal nature. They were familiar with the wind and how it forced the branches of trees in the park behind them to dance like beautiful butterflies and ballerinas searching for heaven above, but to each other, they were simply two strangers who simultaneously stumbled upon another of heaven's gates, at fate's command.

"The North Star," Alexis Claudio pointed out, "Harriet Tubman used it to escape slavery." From below, the mountains created by the smooth waves heard this and praised Harriet, for she agreed to let nature guide her heart. They sensed it pierce through their skin deeper than saw blades on plywood, the very vibration of their quietness allowing them to receive from the ocean water below, with the ballerina trees in the background. The wind, the ocean, and the trees were the perfect ménage à trois, and they were that cross-section where the three hearts met. Alexis could have sworn to hear the waves sing in harmony with the trees.

Why couldn't I have been a tree or the wave of the ocean? I'd provide the therapeutic atmosphere to all that opens up to it, Alexis wondered.

"A perfect art is what I'd be if I were to die here and the waves carried my body away in song." When this was said out loud, the moon looked at the North Star, and for a second, a spark almost made its way down.

Were the moon and the star understanding enough to know I wanted to be part of the magic that was nature dressed in midnight? Alexis wondered.

"Shooting star," Ashton Blingston said, "Make a wish," and before a wish was made, they'd gaze at this phoenix from the midnight sky until it reached that septum in their hearts, reminding them for a second of what it was like to have a heart that was not cold.

"I wish for my death to be the most magical and naturefull," Alexis replied. Ashton's eyes which contained pain, danger, secrets, love, and lust were fixed upon Alexis. The calmness of isolated regions of the ocean bed judged them, but their judgments were accepted because they were clueless to the peace that came with being them—a peace, they, the cold hearts, were forced to envy from lonely sidelines. Calmness that could turn seconds into hours and death into freedom.

"My wish is for you to let me give you the entire world," Ashton said.

The ocean screamed, the waves became hazardous snow mountains, and the trees made a 180-degree turn and headed for hell's door instead. Alexis and Ashton knew why they were furious. The world was them, and they were more than gifts to be handed, especially by someone who only knew them from a visual perspective.

"Kill me," Alexis ordered, and the wind brought colder waves ashore. It was not sadness, but instead acceptance. Down below, as the waves prepared to be flattened, to make space, they couldn't help but toss out all the confused, empty, broken hearts that looked like they were preserved by use of fermentation for way too long—crimes committed by those who lived above, like them.

"I'll kiss you instead," Ashton replied, and everything seemed to move backward when this promise was accomplished a few seconds after being made. At the conclusion of the kiss, with the North Star as a witness, as the moon prepared to shine a light sharp enough to cut through the ice that surrounded their cold hearts, upside down seized control; Alexis ended the kiss and let go, falling backward into a consistently dreamt fantasy for eternity. Among the rotten hearts that remained in the waves' possession, Alexis's lay calmly, blessed by the fallen tears of Ashton. Where the waves did not dare to stay, where butterflies and ballerinas dared to never imagine, and cold hearts were forced to adapt, lava became Alexis's final destination—a destination where midnight begins but never ends.

"Tell me," an older man with long silver hair began, at Alexis' arrival, "how could you enjoy living the same night in a loop when it ends in a rain of fire?"

"While the park and pier remain frozen in time here and get destroyed in an endless loop by rains of fire, the stars, the moon, and the waves aren't. The peace they bring is worth dying for," Alexis replied. This amazed the silver-haired man.

This one is unique, the silver-haired man thought, and Alexis heard his thoughts out loud. No one ever considered being in Destination Two the same as being freed.

22

Tales of Spider's Sins

For decades, stories of one of my destinations, Destination Two, had shifted into many forms, until all of those shifts became the product of two final shifts, bad or good. The majority of the people who had the pleasure of hearing about Tri-Rail F know that Destination Two, like all my other destinations, is a place of escape and true happiness. But there were the minority that thought of Destination Two as the worst place that ever existed, an impenetrable prison like no other. If many knew the origin of Destination Two as I do, they'd disagree.

* * * * *

Alfonzo Ramos stepped off the train and walked toward the large steel gate. After the gate opened, Ramos expected to see cages, wild beasts of all kinds, barbarians with whips, a gigantic red guy with long red horns and a tail, along with everything else that scary movies are phenomenal at depicting; but instead, Ramos saw the most beautiful sight ever—waterfalls, rivers with flying fish that were gifted with angelic voices, beautiful apple trees with fruit so ripe one needed to keep their eyes away to prevent salivation. There were tiny houses made of straw, like the old days. There was no one to instruct him, but somehow Ramos knew which house belonged to him. It was like an invisible force was guiding him toward it. When inside, Ramos could not believe his eyes. *How in the hell*, he wondered, as he examined everything. From the inside, one may think he was in a palace—a four-bedroom house made entirely by nature's hand. *This is really magical*, Ramos thought.

Everything inside was wooden. There was a kitchen with fridge, countertop, oven, and everything else you would find inside, but there were no cords attached, so they should not have been operational. A king-size bed, a hot tub made from logs, a shower with a floating wooden sprinkler. *The rumors weren't true*, Ramos thought later that night before he lay in his plant-based, comfortable bed and closed his eyes to sleep.

The next morning, at exactly 6:66 a.m. on the wooden clock that hung on the wall of every room in the wooden straw house, a siren sound woke Ramos. *666*, Ramos wondered and ran outside to see where the sound came from. As soon as he opened the door, rays of red lights blinded him. When Ramos opened his eyes, he looked up and saw the clouds, they gathered and made a gigantic seven. "What's happening?" he asked before he examined where he was.

He was no longer near the house of straws. He was outside his aunt's house, and the time was not random. It was the day he murdered his aunt's husband, Tommy.

"Suck it!" he watched himself scream before Tommy kneeled down to obey. Ramos pulled the trigger and ended Tommy's life. After Tommy's body hit the ground, Ramos watched the clouds above separate and then began to transform into something else entirely.

No, Ramos thought as the clouds turned into lava and headed down toward him. "Ahhhh!" Ramos screamed when the lava touched his skin, but it did not destroy it. It burned like nothing he'd ever imagined, and he wished it burned him into ashes because that would have been an escape from the pain, but that did not happen. As the lava burned his skin, the tissue kept regenerating at a lightning speed, making certain that Ramos felt every burn. After a few minutes, the lava returned to clouds and transformed into a six.

Betronio Olson held Giovanni Salvador tightly and forced him to watch, as Ramos beat his former lover, Carina Davis, and then raped her in front of him. *My son*, Ramos thought regretfully, as he watched on. The clouds transformed after the memory faded, and the second time, instead of turning into lava, they turned into snow.

Ramos screamed in agony when the snowflakes pierced through his skin like shurikens. When the clouds transformed into a five, Ramos tried to predict his next milestone regret. Ramos watched as a French hunter, Aubert Bartholome, and a version of him from a lifetime ago, dragged three tied-up children deep into a wood at midnight and then plunged a dagger into each of their hearts, as the demigod Adameous Orionis watched with a sinister smile. *Technically that is not my sin to pay for*, Ramos thought and hoped something listened right before the clouds transformed from a five to a million sharp little daggers. "Please! I can't take any more! Someone help me!" Ramos begged as the little daggers chopped his skin bit by bit.

"Spot a spider in a web and you shall escape Destination Two," Adamis's voice echoed in Ramos's head as he braced himself for transformation four. The clouds transformed into a four, and Ramos found himself standing face-to-face with three brothers who used to bully his deceased best friend, Betronio Olson. John, Jonas, and Johnny Dynasty all met the bullets of the guns held by Alfonzo's gang members, but it was Ramos who ordered the merciless hit on the triplets in an attempt to gain Betronio's undying loyalty. After the brothers hit the ground, the clouds turned into a rain of snakes, which included black mambas, tiger snakes, inland taipans, *Echis carinatus*, and king cobras. All the snakes fought for Ramos's eye sockets. Ramos's desperation forced him to search his environment for a spider in a web, but he spotted none. The clouds transformed into the number three, and Ramos found himself back to what used to be his mansion for prostitutes, people he kidnapped and then forced to be his slaves. He remembered the night. He stepped out of his car in front of his burning mansion and found himself at the mercy of a bullet, compliment of Giovanni whom he loved more than anyone. Giovanni came closer and pointed a hunting rifle at Ramos's head, one he'd stolen from his girlfriend's father.

"I can't. I—" Giovanni cried after being overwhelmed with flashbacks of all the time Ramos was the father he never had despite horrible methods. And then he took a bullet to the back of the head by Betronio Olson who arrived on the scene late. Ramos reached for his pistol, which Giovanni had caused him to forget he had on him and fired at Betronio's neck. Still there was no spider. After Betronio landed on the ground, the clouds transformed into an ocean, and Alfonzo found himself drowning repeatedly until the clouds transformed into the number two. The memory relived in two confused Ramoses; it was something he only experienced in a dream, as far as he was concerned. He was without the slightest idea that it was a memory from another reality. Ramos set a plan in motion and met Betronio in an old house of his and put a bullet through his brain.

This has to be the spider in the web, Ramos thought after Betronio's body fell on the tall grass, right before the clouds began to change again. Without control, Ramos's body floated up in the air. Suspended in midair, Ramos watched as the clouds transformed into a storm of lightning, and after he was roasted enough, the clouds changed into an army of vultures. "Ahhhhh! Help! Please!" Ramos screamed as the flying vultures ate him like a barbecue feast, and yet no one listened. The clouds changed into one, and the memory played was the most recent to Ramos, but he did not remember it. Ramos wheeled into his bedroom and waited for his friend Jesse to prepare his bed and then help him settle down.

After Jesse walked out, Ramos turned the lights back on and uncapped a bottle of fentanyl. "I am so sorry, my dear Jesse," Ramos said and swallowed as many pills as his mouth allowed and then forced his eyes closed. After Ramos watched his own eyes close, the clouds transformed again into a five-year-old Alfonzo Ramos crying in a dark corner.

"What's wrong, little one?" Ramos asked his child self, and the five-year-old boy looked up with eyes as wet as the ocean that repeatedly drowned Ramos in one of his previous numbers.

"It's so cold," the little boy replied and then transformed into an ice breeze. As if it had a mind of its own, the icy breeze, which Ramos saw with his naked eyes, entered through Ramos's nose and journeyed all the way to his heart, which it then made as hard as marble.

After dealing with the agony that came with having marble for a heart, Ramos watched the clouds transform back into the number seven. "Nooo! Help me, please! I promise to be better! I don't belong here!" By what felt like the seventh spin of the seven stages of what he considered his hell, Ramos finally spotted something he thought was unusual.

Spider in a web, Ramos thought, relieved, as he carefully studied the night of Giovanni's death. The bullet that came from Betronio's gun, the one he used to kill Giovanni changed by spin. Thanks to his years dealing drugs, selling guns, and robbing police officers, Ramos gained enough knowledge on weapons to recognize that the bullet changed from a 9 mm to 9 mm +P after leaving the gun and before hitting Giovanni. "I spotted the spider in the goddamn web!' Ramos shouted at the clouds, proudly, before they transformed into the ocean again, and then everything went dark.

"Where am I?" Ramos wondered. There was not a single sign of light. Like a blind man, Ramos began to navigate through the darkness, and then at the sudden sound of Jesse's voice screaming.

"Alfi! Please come back to me! I can't lose you!" a little light appeared. Ramos followed the light until it became bigger and bigger. Out of the darkness, Ramos opened his eyes, and there he was, in a hospital bed. It reminded him of when he was so little again.

Was it all a dream again? Ramos wondered as Jesse looked into his awakened eyes with gratitude. "What happened?" Ramos asked and spotted his wheelchair in a corner in the hospital room.

"You overdosed. You died! It's a miracle!" Jesse told him, rejoicing and shocked at the same time.

Spot a spider in a web, and you shall escape Destination Two, a voice echoed in Ramos's head.

Thank you, Adamis, Ramos thought.

23

Tales of Waves' Final Call

Jared Robinson's tears were enough to float a nation. She deemed it fair considering how long he withheld them. When Jackie Bernes, Jared's therapist, looked into his eyes and witnessed the slow collapsing dam behind his cornea, it almost made her grow wings and fly to a place where the body of water could not follow, if such a place even existed. But Jackie understood where all the pain came from.

"I suggest you do call," Jackie advised as Jared left her office that afternoon. Jared partially obeyed; he grabbed the phone from the wall when he arrived home.

At least I am able to touch the phone, Jared told himself. *That's a step forward.*

Ever since Jared had heard the voicemail five days before, only his wife and daughter had used the phone at all. The terrifying thought of accidentally picking up a call from Adam Bryce had kept him at bay. Jared played the voicemail over and copied the number into a piece of paper before hanging the phone back on the wall.

After dinner, Jared said good night to his wife, Pamilla, and his daughter, Ashelyn, and rushed out of the house into the windy night—not, of course, without his long-sleeve camo jacket, the keys to his Suzuki AEM carbon fiber Hayabusa, and his backpack, which had in it his cellphone, a bottle of eucalyptus oil, a flashlight, and his favorite photo album.

On the parking lot next to his favorite nature trail, a few feet away from the beach, Jared parked his bike and walked toward his chosen spot. What was astounding about the heavenly nature trail was that, despite its being part of one of the many entrances to the local beach, Jared was certain less than a hundred people actually knew of its existence and its true beauty. Uncaring about what might have been crawling about on the sand, Jared sat down and used two rocks to focus the light of his flashlight. With the peaceful sounds of the dancing ocean waves in the background, Jared turned to the first page of the photo album that highlighted the beginning of the tearful moment that had been bestowed on him by fate at age forty-six.

The first picture, a simple photo of his father, Mason Robinson, teaching him how to build a castle made of sand at six years old, on this same very beach was how it all began.

"When this Operator guy calls people, why doesn't he give them the chance to say goodbye to their family?" Jared asked his father who was telling him about a magical being that was rumored to have descended on earth and built magical trains to places of refuge where the impossible was made possible.

"Well, there are some rumors that he only makes that exception for special people," his father replied, and then a shadow cast itself before the two of them.

Jared looked up to see, and he saw a little boy who looked the same age as he. "I am Adam, and I want to play with you and your castle."

Mason stood up and made up an excuse to get away. Fate had finally presented his little boy with a chance to make a friend for the first time since they had moved two years before, and he did not want to ruin it. As Mason assumed, fate was at work, and the two little boys bonded well and became friends.

"We will become friends and best friends after. We will stop being friends when the ocean waves break and stops dancing," Adam told Jared, as his mom walked over to get him.

So young and wise, Mason thought as he watched Adam and his mother walk away. *I just hope he never changes.*

The second picture was a photo of Jared and Adam smiling in the arms of Mason, at Jared's eleventh birthday party. "Do you know what this birthday means for you?" Mason had asked Jared in front of his family and Adam.

"I am almost twelve and will finally dance at *Young Stars To-Be*!" Jared said excitedly.

"It's a yearly competition," Mason explained, "that is hosted every December 1 and limited to only twelve-year-olds. Three top dancers are picked and are sent to Los Angeles and eventually are made into the famous dancers we know today."

That made Adam curious. "I want to do that, too, Mr. Robinson. Make us stars together!" Adam begged.

Mason agreed, and for almost an entire year, he took the two boys into the nature trail, sprayed eucalyptus in the air, played Journey or Cher on his portable radio and showed them his best dancing moves.

The third picture was a photo of Jared, with crutches, standing next to Adam who held a first-place *Young Stars To-Be* medal, with the brightest smile on his face. Just three days prior to the competition, Colby Kurk, the bully at their school, decided to target Adam. Jared had stepped in between them, in defense of his friend, and stood his ground as his father always said to do. One attempted, miscalculated pull by Colby sent Jared crushing to the ground, and his knee joint paid the price.

When Jared turned to the fourth picture, the wind intensified, spreading the smell of eucalyptus. *Why,* Jared wondered as he stared at the picture, *did you become famous and forget about me?*

He had never bothered to read the letter, but before he tossed it out, Jared had taken a picture of the goodbye letter Adam wrote and left the neighbor to give to Jared and his dad the next time they visited.

"They wanted me to tell you guys that saying goodbye was too hard," Adam's neighbor said, knifing a corner of Jared's heart that had never entirely healed.

"*Why?*" Jared had wondered aloud before his father hugged and told him, "You'll make a new and better friend, bud."

Jared closed the picture album and picked up his cell phone again. With the sounds of the wind, whispering trees, and the ocean waves mixing in harmony in the background, Jared inhaled and exhaled the eucalyptus scent and remembered the voicemail.

"Hey Jare… I am terribly sick. Doctors said I was not going to make it through the year. Hopeless, I was giving away valuable items when I stumbled upon the picture we took the night of the competition. I had forgotten about writing your house number on the back and do not even know if you guys still have that phone. Anyway, that guy your dad always told us stories about is real, and he called me. He will rescue me. He gave me a few hours to say goodbye to people I deem special. This is where my journey ends, Jare, and I could not think of anyone I'd rather hear in this moment. Please return my call before the Operator calls again, and let's hear each other's voice one final time. I am sorry. I never stopped caring."

Jared felt his tears coming, cold as ice. As the last of the tears rolled down his cheek, Jared listened but could no longer hear the sound of the dancing ocean waves.

Adam Bryce, one of the greatest and best-known dancers of his time sat close to the phone and awaited a call. The phone rang two times. Adam relived his most cherished memories, took a deep breath, and then picked up. "Hello," Adam said to the caller on the opposite end.

24

Tales of Another's Reality

Giovanni Ramos looked in the mirror and smiled. Standing next to him was his happy girlfriend, Carina Olson. "You're becoming such a man. Your father will be proud when you go out there and he sees the man you've become," Carina said. She kissed Giovanni on the cheek and then left the room. Through the looking glass, Giovanni watched someone else walk in a few seconds after Carina walked out. It wasn't just anyone; it was the demigod Adameous Orionis, a man Giovanni never thought he'd seen so soon after their last encounter.

"Adam," Giovanni said. *He must've come to collect*, Giovanni thought.

"It's Adameous, Adam was my father from ages ago," Adameous corrected. "And, yes, I did come to finally collect on your wish."

"I thought when you said you'd ask for payment later, you meant years, not two weeks," Giovanni stated, and Adameous gave him a sinister laugh.

"When you wished for the hottest young lady in your school to only ever have eyes for you, I made it happen in seconds, with the snap of a finger, so either agree to pay the price now or watch your life fall apart bit by bit till death is your only way to ease the pain." Before Giovanni had a chance to respond, Adameous added,

"Besides you probably have the easiest payment compared to many people whose wishes I've granted."

"What's your price?" Giovanni asked.

"Starting in the next half hour, I want you to give me absolute control of your body and mind. Let it be a temporary possession," Adameous demanded.

"How long is temporary?"

"If my calculations are right, only about six months," Adameous finished.

Though Giovanni did not understand what Adameous meant by calculations, and though it pained him that he was going to watch his father's wedding through the eyes of a stranger, he knew that it was better than the alternative.

"Deal. Yes," Giovanni said.

* * * * *

Dear Adamis,

 It is I, Adameous. My brother, I wanted to inform you of the recent accomplishments in our prophecies, many of them I've made come to light. However, brother, I will need your assistance on the next one on the list. I've traveled all of the realities, and none of them present any trusting possibilities of Alfonzo Ramos journeying to Destination Four. Brother, I've come up with a plot.

 You see, in this corrupted reality, reality 750, Alfonzo Ramos is a faithful, religious father with a dark past, and I am going to explain how we'll go about using those things to our advantage. Brother, use your skills and become Alfonzo Ramos's former nemesis in this reality, Reyman Debroyi, a man whose girlfriend Alfonzo stole and whose father he murdered. Reyman committed suicide after he lost his dad; however, no one is aware. See you soon, brother.

Yours truly, Adameous

After he finished, Adameous Orionis sealed the envelope with the letter inside and sent it away with the wind.

* * * * *

Suited, Alfonzo Ramos stood at the altar, next to his son, Giovanni Ramos. Alfonzo had no words to describe how he felt. Every cell in his body impatiently waited for his love, Jasmine, to appear before them. When Jasmine appeared, after what felt to Alfonzo like a century-long wait, someone pushed her, and she landed on her face.

Alfonzo locked eyes with a ghost from his past, a man he had heard rumors had taken his own life. "Reyman," Alfonzo forced himself to say, scared.

"Get down!" someone yelled before Reyman pulled out a gun and fired at Alfonzo. Alfonzo wanted to get out of the way, but he froze. After the shot, Reyman ran off, not having stayed long enough to know that Giovanni had jumped in front of Alfonzo.

"Gio, no, no, don't close your eyes," Alfonzo begged as he used his two hands to try to stop his son's bleeding. "You shouldn't have…," Alfonzo began to cry when the blood wouldn't stop.

"I love you, Dad," Giovanni forced himself to say before his eyes closed shut.

* * * * *

Alfonzo Ramos stood in a crossroad with a dead serpent and waited to meet the infamous Adameous Orionis. Alfonzo was a religious man and only believed in one true God, until his hands were tied. "I am betraying all my beliefs being here, so can you just show up so we can get this over with?" Alfonzo yelled.

Alfonzo remembered saying something similar to the old lady at the corner store by his house when he went to her to find out if there was any way to bring back the dead.

"Kill a serpent at an isolated crossroads on the fifth night of any month, and a beautiful man by the name of Adameous Orionis will give you one wish," she'd told him. "However, do remember there's a price for every good deed."

As Alfonzo remembered that moment, a light flashed before his eyes. Adameous appeared finally. "What's your wish, sir?" he asked Alfonzo.

"I was led to believe you can read minds, so is there a point in saying it out loud?" Alfonzo began. "Just tell me what price I must pay to get my son, Gio, back."

Alfonzo thought back to the day of his wedding, the day he lost his son, Giovanni. Alfonzo never expected a nemesis from eight years before to resurface on his happiest day and make it his saddest. *That was indeed an asshole move on Reyman's part*, Alfonzo thought.

"If you kill someone's father, he will get revenge," Adameous interrupted. "It doesn't matter how long it takes."

Feeling invaded, Alfonzo said, "I came here for a wish, not therapy, so can you please get on with my price so I don't have to deal with you false gods any longer."

"False, yet it's me you came to. Your belief is the price," Adameous told Alfonzo right before he touched his forehead and took him back to his ongoing feud with Reyman Debroyi, a former drug-dealer friend of Alfonzo's who turned on him after Alfonzo started dating his former lover, Jasmine Cartaret.

Adameous took Alfonzo to a specific night; Jasmine had taken Alfonzo to church for the very first time, and Reyman had followed them there with a gun. His target was not Alfonzo. Reyman fired two times at Jasmine and ran off. Alfonzo was left with a bloody Jasmine in his arms, and he was afraid she would not make it. Desperate, Alfonzo turned to every cross in the church, and for the very first time, he prayed.

Jasmine lived; it was a miracle big enough to convince Alfonzo that he was wrong for having been an atheist before meeting Jasmine.

"How can you take someone's belief?" Alfonzo asked Adameous after he was shown that night again.

"Easy. I want your memories from that entire day and from today," Adameous demanded. "Give me a yes, and you won't remember believing in God, ever meeting a demigod, and your son, Gio, will be back home waiting for you as if he never died."

"Yes," Alfonzo said.

* * * * *

Alfonzo Ramos stood on the green field alongside what seemed like thousands of others, with his ticket in hand—train number four. Up until the point where he was forced by a bunch of creatures he couldn't understand, Ramos did not remember believing in magical beings or a tri-rail. After his train finally arrived and he was inside, many conversations began between the two he sat with and others around them. "I regret not having believed in this tri-rail my whole life," a lady who sat across from them said.

"I was an atheist my whole life, but being in this train is evidence gods do exist," one of the two guys who sat next to her added.

"So was I," Alfonzo joined in finally, "but if we didn't believe in the God who owns this magical train that 'goes to places beyond imagine,' then why not cast us out of the 'need to be rescued' list?" After he finished, everyone else who had not been involved in the conversation turned their attention toward him.

"My therapist once told me that not believing in anything is a belief in its own," one of the two ladies whom Alfonzo sat between said.

"Like all of you, the only thing I believed in was that science was behind everything," the other lady said, "but now that I am here and see all of this and based on what I heard happens after, I must say this is one cruel God we are dealing with."

Everyone turned to her for elaboration.

"When I was little, my grandma always told me about all of this, including the dark secrets about other realities."

Everyone seemed confused about the other reality statement.

"There's more than one reality?" the guy across from them asked, and she nodded.

"Tri-rail F is one. However I was told stories about an original reality that splits into many more. I hear every time someone in that original reality messes with fate or time, a whole new reality is created."

"How could that even work?" Alfonzo asked. "All these people from all those realities going to just four destinations and yet no one ever spoke about clones when talking about the tri-rail."

"You see, that's where it gets cruel. If someone from one of those secondary realities journeys to Tri-Rail F first, then they stay stuck in limbo until their original reality version goes there, too, and after the original goes to Tri-rail F, all the 'clones' become simply dreamlike memories."

Alfonzo could tell from their faces that she had scared everyone in the train who sat close enough to have heard.

"Who said we are not living in the original reality?" Alfonzo forced himself to ask.

"We might be. I am just saying it's cruel and that I won't be surprised if we're not."

After she said that, not a soul in the train spoke until arrival.

"Go in," one of the ice creatures told Alfonzo after their arrival. It was a plain field with nothing but dirt and one huge white door. After Alfonzo walked in with the others, they all vanished, and it was just him in an empty hallway. Alfonzo walked straight until he came up to a line made only by versions of himself. They all stood there motionless and speechless, and right as he was about to speak, Alfonzo lost his voice. When he tried to turn and run back, his foot felt glued to the floor. Then his sight disappeared.

25

Tales of Sus Sueños

There are those who say dreams are memories of another lifetime. And according to a few, they are memories of another existence, one that was almost parallel to our own. Like many people, at first Paola Alanis did not know what her dreams meant either. And then she had her first dream of me. Like everyone else on the chess board that is Earth, I kept a close eye on Paola for years before the dreams began. In fairness, I was more interested in the baby that Paola was destined to give birth to. Paola did not know this, and it would be ages until she did, but Paola was destined to give birth to Earth's greatest hero, Alfonzo Ramos. Alfonzo had taken many forms through the years, ever since the beginning of time. But unlike all the mothers who helped in contributing to the reincarnation cycle of Alfonzo's life, Paola was destined to be the last mother before all the prophecies were accomplished, prophecies about Alfonzo saving men from all that was considered and named "bad."

On a visit to a beach bar in Santo Domingo, the capital of the Dominican Republic, from her birthplace of Hato Mayor, Paola and her best friend, Yanez, ran into three thieves who believed the two girls had come from wealthy families and wanted them to pay a ransom to avoid fatal conflicts. "Please, Paola, give them all of it," Yanez begged, but Paola stood her ground and held her hand purse tightly and refused to give in.

Paola remembered everything her aunt said to her when she was ten and was sent to sell freshly harvested fruits and vegetables to the nearest outdoor marketplace and had been bullied into giving them away. "If you ever let someone take our hard-earned harvest again because you're too weak to fucking fight back, you'll feel worse than this!" her aunt yelled before slapping her across the face more times than Paola was ever able to count.

When Paola made the mistake again, she remembered how cold it felt when her aunt forced her to sleep outside on their farm for three consecutive days, to toughen her up.

It worked. After the cold days of sleeping outside on their farm, Paola had finally gotten to where her aunt wanted her to be as far as the world was considered.

"You'll have to get it. Over my dead body!" Paola said through clenched teeth, as one of the guys aimed his gun at her forehead.

"No. Please don't do this!" Yanez screamed. "Someone help us please!" Yanez screamed some more and began to cry louder.

Bang! Bang!

"You think we're fucking around now?" One of the guys said, his sleeveless shirt covered in blood after Paola watched Yanez's body hit the ground. Paola watched on without breaking, as the guy who murdered her best friend pushed the other guy aside and aimed his gun at her forehead instead.

"Over my dead body," she repeated, and before he pulled the trigger, something swung by and took off his head, nearly hitting Paola's throat in the process. It was a machete. The other two guys escaped, but behind the guy who had rescued Paola stood a bunch of people.

What is this? she wondered before she examined each and every one of them individually. Her aunt had told her stories of a hero who lived in secret and helped many people escape the harsh living conditions of the Dominican Republic illegally. "He helps them go to better places like America, England, Puerto Rico, and Tri-Rail F," her aunt explained whenever she spoke of him, "But he only finds you if you're lucky and in distress while being where he is. If you ever run into him, don't waste the opportunity of a lifetime, my child. Journey with him."

"Without you?" Paola remembered asking.

"Yes, I'd prefer one of us getting out than none of us. Plus, I promised your mom I'd always do what I thought was best when it came to protecting you and your sister," she said. "She listened, and so you have to follow her steps if you're ever given the chance."

Paola looked at the group of people and forced the question out. "Are you Fabian Ramos, the ocean rescuer?"

He nodded.

She was far from disappointed; he had the body of the godly man her sister and aunty always bragged about. His arms, strong and filled with veins, which fought to reveal themselves, were enough to support his legend. He looked as though he used those arms for anything and everything. "Wow," Paola said, and the entire crowd just stared at her, but it was not mutual. While they studied her, she studied him—his beautiful and yet dangerous brown eyes and his shoulder-length curly hair. His physique and features made her wonder if he was even Dominican.

"The one and only. Now, please, move aside and let us continue on," he said, and it almost made her sweat. English was not his first language; his thick accent gave it away.

No wonder all of these people chose to let him lead them, she thought as she listened to the echoes of his dominant voice, which matched his assertive personality.

"Please let me come with you. I am completely done here." After Paola begged, she waited for him to say no, and if he said yes, she waited for his conditions. Living up to his authoritative reputation, he turned and looked at the crowd for their input and in unity, they all nodded.

"Stay with the herd," he told her, and she obeyed.

The journey took three months. Their destination was a beach site in Monte Cristi, but during one of their nights on the way, Paola overheard two older women speak about Fabian.

"I hear both of his parents were born in Puerto Rico and moved to Salcedo and then were killed in a break-in when he was only three months old," the oldest of the two women said, and Paola listened carefully for the other to respond.

"So tragic. Poor child. One good thing came out of it. He helps others," said the other.

"Florida is our first destination. The journey will be far and long, so brace yourselves," Fabian told them the next morning, and although Paola had no clue where she wanted to go, she suspected if it was one of the stops made by someone like Fabian, then it would be a great choice. Sadly, before the boat filled with travelers made it to Florida, a wild storm created by my own hands overtook the tides. The only survivors, Fabian and Paola, eventually made it to shore, and luckily for them, Fabian had an old friend whom he had helped cross over who was more than happy to provide them with a temporary home. The stories of the heroic Fabian ended with that storm. The only thing Fabian cared about after the incident was the beautiful Paola whom he fell in love with after a few months. Fabian and Paola, with the help of a few friends of Fabian's, cheated the system and eventually got a place on their own, and with that new place came a marriage proposal that Paola could not reject for all the world. The next step in this was, of course, marriage. Both Paola and Fabian spent their entire lives dreaming of having a big family; however, when the time came, the two learned that they were both infertile. And then one night, Paola had a dream like no other.

In her dream, Paola found herself near a beautiful lake she and her best friend used to go to where they practiced playing their violins. She heard a peaceful tune and followed it. When she arrived, she saw me. I had my back turned toward her; I was finishing a beautiful portrait of my past lover, and when she called out Fabian's name, I turned around and revealed myself.

I've never seen this man before, she thought. "Who are you?"

To her, I was the most beautiful being she'd ever laid eyes on. It made her curious. It awoke her hormones. I could see she was fighting to keep herself in check, but I also knew it was not going to last long. *How can one man be this beautiful?* she thought, and then added, *Stop thinking this way, it's cheating.*

"I am the demigod Adameous Orionis," I told her.

"How'd you end up in my dreams?" she said.

At least she knew she was dreaming, I admitted to myself, *most of them never discover that part.*

"Well, usually someone who craves something badly tends to be here. I grant wishes. You have a wish that destiny would like to see come true," I lied and hoped she'd believe it.

"What wish?" she asked, and deep inside her mind, I knew she had already given herself the answer before she even asked the question.

"To always keep the one you love. The only way to do that is to give him a child," I told her, and she seemed shocked, as if I had just read her mind. I had.

Before she gave me an answer, she looked past me and toward my canvas. "Is she the reason you're taking care of people like me?" she asked, and I tried to read her mind to know why she asked that question, and surprisingly, it was one of the two times that my mind-reading powers had failed me. It was as if they were nonexistent.

"I know a thing or two about art. Sometimes the art is a reflection of the artist and how they're feeling," Paola began; there was an honesty to her voice. I did not need to read her mind to know she was speaking truthfully. "You made her eyes look like snowflakes, but I can tell that they're just really wet. She was crying a lot. How did she die?" she asked.

"Enough of that. If you want your wish to be true, you must sleep with me," I explained. "Nothing is free, and you know you want to."

"But my husband. That'd be cheating," she replied, but in her mind, she had already surrendered. She just needed a little push.

"It's just a dream," I told her. She took her time, but she came closer to me. Before our lips joined, she said lustily that she was a lucky woman.

Two days after the encounter, after she woke up from the mysterious dream she was never able to explain, she told Fabian the good news.

"I'm pregnant!" she screamed from the bathroom. He had doubts that it was his, but when blood tests came back to reveal that it was his, they named their beautiful child together.

"Alfonzo Ramos," they both agreed.

26

Tales of Last Dream

My first life, a trail mix of reality and fantasy, was a roller-coaster ride, but the end was happy. Though I'd be lying if I said I could go back and pick out the fantasies from the realities, one thing I know for certain is, it was the fantasies that really made it a life worth living.

I was sitting in the middle of two guys who seemed the same age as I; we were heading to a fairy tale, a mystery we knew nothing of yet.

"I can't believe this is real!" said the guy to my right. There was a ton of excitement in his voice. We were on a train, but this train was far from ordinary. It was beyond magical, as was its promised destination.

"Fairy tales are real," the other one replied, half asleep. The train ride was long, so I had already gotten to hear the stories of how each of them came to know of the man in charge of the magical trains, a mysterious being named the Operator. The first time I heard of him was from a patient at the hospital where I worked in Atlanta, Georgia. His organs were shutting down, and everyone knew he was not going to live to tell the tale of being run down on the streets by his girlfriend's ex-boyfriend.

"All I pray for is a miracle!" I'd heard him scream to the ceiling when he thought he was alone. "So much for some savior. The

Operator, my ass. He won't save me," he told his girlfriend, who spent the whole visit with wet eyes.

I did my research on The Operator and learned of his legend, a legend that was said to have originated in the Dominican Republic. The legend speaks of a mysterious godlike being who built a magical tri-rail with four magical trains that journeyed to places beyond dreams. It also says if you're lucky, he'll call you in times of need and set you free from Earth. *So much for that,* I thought after I heard that the poor boy died, and no magical being called him.

Later on in life, I learned that the Operator was not a made-up tale after all.

It was December 1 of the year 2088. I was ninety-one years old. I had an album full of memories—old pictures of everyone I'd had the opportunity of meeting and loving the entirety of my life. I looked at it every night before bed. After I did this that night, with Celine Dion's song, "Encore un Soir," playing in the background, I began to prepare my bed for rest, and that's when my phone began to ring.

"Reyman Debroyi?" the unfamiliar voice asked.

"Yes, it is he," I replied.

"The Operator has chosen you for one of his magical trains. Sleep tonight, enjoy your final dream, and await his instructional call by morning. Speak of this to no soul," the stranger on the phone ordered.

I finished my bed and laid my head down. I could not remember anything more than I did, including waking up, until I stepped inside the train. After I tried to force myself to recall if I'd had that final dream, one of the guys whispered in my ear, "Look, here they go."

And I obeyed. I followed his gaze and laid eyes on them. They were the same humanlike creatures we'd seen at the station before we hopped onboard. They were basically humanly designed ice statues that had developed their own civilization beyond Earth. Some of them were unique in the sense that their arteries and veins weren't the same colors. I was a nurse, but none of the science courses I took prepared me for understanding the way their internal organs were structured.

"They're giving some people some type of orange pill," the guy to my left said and lifted his head for a better look.

"According to rumors, the Operator orders them to give those to 'unique' people," the guy to my right explained. "I hear that everyone loses their memories of the old life in two of the four places that the trains go. Apparently they give those magic pills to people to help them create one final dream that they can keep."

"How can one person conjure an entire lifetime into a single dream?" I asked him and awaited an answer, as I studied the faces of those who received the orange pills. One guy was even given two.

"And what if it's a nightmare?" the guy to my left added.

"You'd have to ask the Operator all of that when we meet him. All I know is that ten of these people are luckier than we are," he responded.

Two of the ice crystal creatures walked by our seats with the tiny bag of pills, and then they backed up. "Wait," one of them said to the other, and it surprised everyone around us—the fact that they actually spoke our language. "You!" he finished and reached down into the clear plastic bag and reached over to give the pill.

"Me?" I asked with my own index finger pointed at myself.

He nodded and stood there until I swallowed the pill. After the pill went down and I felt it disintegrate, my head began to feel heavy, so much so that it felt as if I was walking with three kendal balls stuck to my upper body. As for my eyes, they fought me, trying to shut, and as hard as I tried, it was a fight that I did not win.

Reyman, open your eyes and be here, a voice echoed in my head, and when I obeyed, I was no longer in the middle of two jocks in a magical train. "My name is Proxy, and the Operator has made it my duty to escort you," an old man with silver hair said. He had eyes so beautiful that they reminded me of a man I once fell in love with instantly because of the spell his eyes cast. The difference though, was that Proxy's pupils were as silver as his long hair. They were not circular; they were snowflakes. He almost looked like one of the creatures from the train, but it seemed as though he'd started the evolutionary process three decades before them.

"To where?" I asked, and he gave me his hand. When I stood on my feet, I looked around and could not believe my eyes. Like a dream, my own, it was as though I shared the eyesight of all the birds that flew above because despite being in one edge of the beautiful garden, I could see every corner of it. "What's this place?" I asked Proxy, whose eyes had changed completely.

"That Place," he replied, and pollen filled the atmosphere.

It can't be, I thought. I remembered the first time I came to That Place and how it was not as vast, nor as beautiful. "That Place was only a fraction of my long imagination growing up," I admitted, and it was the very first time in my ninety-one years of life that I spoke this truth to anyone.

"When it comes to us, everything is possible. You're doing this. We're inside a long-hidden part of your subconscious," Proxy replied, and I still could not believe it.

I turned around and saw the most beautiful waterfall. It was not random though; it looked similar to one my very first lover and I once visited, a memory I had forgotten. *He's right*, I finally admitted, and then a door appeared in the center of the garden, with steps to assist. The medieval iron door had nothing but the other side of the beautiful garden behind it, but I remembered a similar dream I once had. The same door appeared in my dream when I found myself in the middle of the ocean, with no land in sight. It took me three nights, with the same dream before I decided to open the door to see what was on the other side. I did and woke up before it revealed the big mystery. I tried to force myself to have the same dream the fourth night, but it never happened.

"Open it. Let's go enjoy this final fantasy," Proxy suggested.

As I climbed up the steps, the garden began to disappear. It started with all the dandelions transforming and freeing all their feathery bristles to the sky. The water from the waterfall swam backward and then dried out as if it never was there. By the time I got to the last step, my beautiful garden had become a desert. I turned the knob and walked in. Proxy stayed close.

Inside, my clothes had changed completely. I no longer had on jeans and a T-shirt, with Under Armour sneakers. Instead, I had on a three-piece white damask tuxedo with dark-blue print, matching pants, simple white dress shoes, and an ancient Roman-designed black mask. The building resembled an ancient cathedral. I was inside a castle of my own making.

"Let's go," Proxy ordered, and we began to walk down the hall. As the hall came to life, like pictures hung on the wall, the many adventures of mine began to play like a movie. We began to see people. These people weren't strangers. They were everyone who impacted my life.

"Those are milestones," Proxy said as we walked past a live replay of when I first met Dallas Niezao—my first fantasy, my first lover, and many other things.

"I see," I said and remembered we were inside my head. "Guess I never moved on," I admitted. *I was an addict after all*, I thought, *and Dallas was my lifetime favorite drug.* On each side of the wall were my family and friends, all dressed ready for a ball—Victorian ball gowns for all the ladies, and tuxedos of the past for the gentlemen, with matching masks. None were as memorable as the one I wore. In fact they were all clones. At the end of the line they created awaited another double set of anciently constructed doors.

On one side stood Anivens Fazil, a best friend of mine, and on the other my oldest brother Sean Debroyi. "Go in," they said sanctimoniously and then opened the doors to reveal the gigantic ballroom.

"Whoa," I said, and Justin Timberlake's song "Mirrors," my favorite song of all time, stopped playing in the hall. With the conclusion of his song, the double doors closed behind me. The large ballroom was everything I'd construct. The floor was not wooden. Instead it was grassy and beautiful. In every corner and on every wall of the ballroom was a different species of flowers. Another best friend of mine, Amanda Falcon, used to send me pictures of beautiful nature trails she'd visited, and I'd created a whole album for the pictures; and looking at the ballroom, it seemed that someone discovered that album and decided to release all of that beauty inside it. Looking at how beautiful the ballroom was, I felt like a mermaid learning to swim underwater for the very first time. It took my breath away. In the center of the ballroom were a bunch of clones of me. They wore the exact same outfit, and each of them stood next to a past lover of mine. The males all wore vintage Mao collar frock coats in white jacquard fabric with golden embroidery and crystal clasp. And instead of hats, they each had their own silver Roman mask of two pegasi chasing an elegant crest.

As for my past female lovers, they each wore dark-blue short-sleeve Victorian ball gowns, with long black gloves. And on their hands, they each held a mask I once came across in an ancient artifact store. It was a dreamy masquerade mask—silver with small touches of dark-blue sparkles. One side was entirely a butterfly, while the other was just half of an ordinary mask. As "Dancin' Away with My Heart" by Lady Antebellum began to play, each clone of mine approached his appropriate lover. I waited to see which past lover of mine was mine to dance with.

"Dance with me?" someone said behind me. I turned around, and there he was, Mike Everett, my past lover whose eyes no other lover ever matched and whose story ended tragically.

"You all share one mind, but he has all the control," Proxy whispered into my ears as I walked Everett to the dance floor. Proxy pointed toward the middle of the dance floor, and I wished I had not looked. I looked, and after seeing it, I felt I was no longer the unique one of all the clones of me. In the center of the dance floor was another me, but unlike the rest that I called clones, his entire outfit made mine irrelevant, just as that of his dance partner made the others. I felt my mind losing control, and it did. Like the clones, my mind headed toward the center.

I opened my eyes and could hear all the thoughts of the clones of me. By the door, one of them stood out, and he danced with Everett. My dance partner, who wore a red version of the outfit of the other past lovers, had removed his mask and revealed his face to me. "Niezao?" I said, and he smiled.

"I told you we'd end up together in the end," he said and pulled me closer to dance. As we swung each other on the dance floor, I remembered all the stories of my lovers that were blessed with this amazing ballroom. The first, Niezao. I was six, abused verbally at home, bullied at school, and isolated from the world until my imagination gave me the perfect protector. Niezao showed me how to burn myself with ice and salt to avoid feeling emotional pain, taught me how to create a perfect world inside my head that we called That Place that we'd journey to whenever the outside world became too cruel. Niezao and I even eloped, but then he told me he had a rare disease and wouldn't live for long.

We struggled with it and argued a lot about how I wanted to die with him, but during one of the nights of hurricane Irma in 2017, Niezao sneaked out in the night and never returned. He took my heart with him but left me with the ring that witnessed our forever and a letter that breaks my heart every time I look at it. The backlash was harsh. I dealt with an abusive imaginative version of Niezao who tortured me. In the midst of this heartbreak and torture, I fell in love with the beautiful Bianca Von Claire who'd overdose. After that, Shane Flyer, who was my best friend at that time. In an effort to get over this one-sided love, I met Mike Everett. Everett's eyes drew me in. Inside them I always could journey into That Place and hide the way Niezao and I did.

The devilish imagination of Niezao eventually got the best of me and forced me to leave Everett standing outside a building where he took me to a white party where he'd told me he wanted to spend the rest of his life with me. I ended up outside Shane Flyers's front door, and after I finally came out to him about being bisexual and in love with him, he'd say the most hurtful things. At the end of that night, I'd taken the imagination with me and drove my car into a tree. I ended up in a coma instead of dying, and in it, I got engaged to Everett and cheated on him with Shane Flyer. I had a long and complicated life where I lost my wife, Cahya Falcon, who never existed outside my coma; and with our daughter Donatella by my side, I married Shane Flyer and lived a happy life.

Years later, while married to Shane, I learned Everett had taken his own life because I broke his heart. Nearing the end of that coma, Niezao returned as a different person, a darker person, and destroyed that perfect last marriage.

When I woke up from my coma, that's when I finally accepted that Niezao was just an imagination from the very beginning. In the hospital that I woke up in, the nurse informed me that Mike had found me where I drove into the tree and brought me in and then unplugged his beloved grandpa, whom he kept in there for what felt like a decade to finance my coma care instead.

"Where is Mike now?" I remembered asking the nurse, and with a devastated look, she told me, "There was a pandemic, a virus called coronavirus that killed a lot of people. Mike was amongst that unlucky few, but on his deathbed, he ordered his sister to do her best to keep you plugged in. He had faith that one day you'd wake up. I am sorry. He was a hero."

After my coma, after Everett, I thought I'd never fall in love the same way again, and then I had a reunion with Rafeal Rosario, someone whom I met once when I was a prostitute, something I did during the time I was with Niezao, for survival, and then in an attempt to get over Niezao after he left me. I donated a kidney to save Rafeal's life one day, and we fell in love after that. When it came time for us to get married, Rafeal bailed at the last minute and ended us, based on religious myths his grandma used to tell him before bedtime. Having been forced by my parents to grow up a Jehovah's Witness for a huge portion of my life, I understood his choice, but I never loved anyone the same again.

I dated many people after, including Maria Doresmand, another best friend of mine whom I once dated back in middle school and high school, around the times of Niezao and I and Venessa Beginns whom I met through Anivens Facil, but none of them got my heart the way Maria did the first time, the way Niezao did, the way Shane Flyer did, the way Everett, and the way Rafeal did.

On the last ballroom dance, they were all there—those I dated and really liked, those I fell deeply in love with, and those I just loved to a minimum degree. Each dancing with that version of me that made them fall in love. Unsurprisingly, my best version was in the center with Niezao.

"The dream comes to its end when the song ends on its third loop," Proxy whispered into my ears, and I knew all the clones heard it too.

For me, you'll always be eighteen and beautiful and dancing away with my heart," Niezao said, as he stared deeply into my eyes, on the third loop of the song. He knew that was always my favorite line in the song.

"I love you," I said, and all the clones repeated it to a past lover of mine.

"And I you," they all replied like robots.

The song ended, and everything disappeared.

27

Tales of Prophecies

My father always told me, wrongly placing or removing one sentence or word can change a story drastically. How I, Alfonzo Ramos, became the Operator was evidence of the truth behind his warning.

"Welcome to your final destination, Sir Ramos!" an old man with long silver hair said when I stepped off the train. It was not my first time seeing one of his kind. Some had horns, some had flowers, and others had something sticking out of their heads. Their inside organs were visible to the outside world but in a nondisgusting way. They were beautiful walking human ice statues.

The settlers of Destination One, along with all of its natives, were rare and magnificent creatures that the world beyond Destination One would never know or appreciate. All stood strong and focused on the icy sky, which had the colors of the rainbow. It was as if a ton of rainbows had crashed against each other. Before I had a chance to ask what they were all waiting for, an earthquake happened, and then a sea of vivid lights cracked a hole through the rainbow sky, with a tiny glimpse of every color ever known to man.

At the sight of what the lights brought, everyone gasped. Chatters began all around. Not a single soul had seen it coming, not even the twins, Adamis and Adameous Orionis, could have predicted it. The biggest misconception in the most famous tale in history had revealed itself. Aside from everyone being wrong for falsely stating the Operator actually ever physically visited earth, the Operator revealed "himself," and everyone turned out to have been wrong about the sex too.

She was a miraculous, admirable treasure piece. A body like hers, features included, was not born but rather made. I bet it took centuries to perfect. She had a cleft chin, but the size was not exaggerated. It was barely noticeable. Her blonde hair, with droplets of unmelted snow that were the same color as her iris was so long it was bound to reach the warm grassy ground at least three seconds before her foot. Her lips were so red you would think they were bloody, her skin so pale and clear it revealed the small cells of her skin tissue, and the mysteries that lay in the wells that were her pores. Before she reached the grass, the man who pretended to be her first hand, also referred to as Proxy, began to collect her icy wet hair. When her foot finally touched the ground, blood ran through her entire body, and her skin became less pale, and her eyeliner, which seemed a bit brown from up above, appeared blacker than midnight.

"I am she. I am the rescuer to whom you all owe thanks for this magical kingdom. I am the Operator. I am Evelyn!" she screamed from where she stood.

There was a little distance between her and the crowd, but somehow what she said attached itself to the wind, allowing every ear to hear. After the crowd began to cheer and praise her, the ground in front of her began to crack. Before any of them had a chance to see what was expected to be revealed, all except Proxy, the twins, and I fell into a slumber.

"My ruby. Finally!" she said with a joyful smile that would last two seconds before turning wicked. She picked up the red tulip-shaped gemstone from the ground and told Proxy to hold it instead.

She turned and looked at the twins who stood only a few feet in front of me. In the silk sleeping gown, which stopped at her knees, she moved her slim body one motion at a time until she reached the twins, who were still paralyzed due to the shock of her arrival. "My dearest nephews, I know I am not who any of you expected to see, but I am all there is left. You guys wanted Mommy and Daddy, and now I will give you guys the pleasure, but first thank you for being so naive and for finally giving me back that which was taken from me decades ago," she said, pulling them both into her arms at the same time.

Then she let go, revealing a planted ice crystal in each of their hearts. The coldness I felt from her was almost like that of the person who led me to my final journey to Tri-Rail F, my daughter Beverly, who was a child of rape and whom I had no idea was my blood until she snuffed the lights out of me for good, not considering the fact that I was a senior stuck in a wheelchair.

"Those prophecies were all lies," she told the twins when they were both on their knees, with their blood turning the green grass into the same red as her lips. "These were the actual consequences of the prophecies coming about." She waved an ancient book in front of their dying eyes.

Later, I'd learn that inside the book were events that had taken place in the lives of normal people. These prophecies were:

"The day the fifth child of a mother forbidden by fate to have children bore three cousins and siblings." This talked about a man who was naive enough to let Adameous trick him into wishing for five kids when he only wanted one, all because he was greedy for money. One of the kids whom Adameous also used to transfer into three bodies to seduce three sisters and have children with them.

"Faith becomes the heart's greatest adversary." This concerned a guy who gave up the love of his life all because his grandmother told him he wouldn't have been chosen for Destination One if he married another man.

"'Reflections stain the heart' talked about a man whose reflection turned him into his worst self and even made him murder once or twice. It was my former best friend Betronio Olson that this prophecy referred to. Although when we were teenagers and he told me about this experience, I never believed it. I never believed his reflection came to life and controlled him.

"'Guilt and loneliness bore a child.' This one spoke of a lady who had an abortion and then started to imagine what having that child would have been like.

"'Grief rewinds time.'" This one was a bit sad to me. It spoke of two best friends. One committed suicide, and Adameous took another form, handed the one who was left a magical notebook that allowed him to spend an entire day with the friend he lost. At the end of it, the friend who committed suicide used the magical notebook and rewrote their history, forcing them to have never even met.

"'Destinations are found without trains.' A prophecy that spoke of a little girl who traveled to the otherside, not through some white light or a door but through the ocean, with a mermaid by her side. I also knew this girl. She was the daughter of Bohen Jones, who was brother to Lisa Jones, a great friend and business partner of mine.

"'Father beds his son and daughter.' This one talked about a cheater who tried to outsmart Adameous and in the process slept with his own daughter who was born a boy and transformed into a girl by a wish he stole from Adameous.

"'Sins consume a house of seven.' I was also linked to this one. The sins were of the Whites, family of a former friend of mine, a friend who ended up murdering them.

"'Feelings and destinations meet contradictions.' This prophecy made me question everything about the destinations. It spoke of someone who saw Destination Two as freedom and another who thought of Destination One as a prison.

"'Waves are forgotten' told the story of two young dancers who agreed to be famous together, one got injured, lost his way, and got forgotten by the other who became famous.

"'And icy heart journeys five of six destinations' told about me and all my death or near-death experiences. No one had ever cheated death as many times as I, I learned.

"The ice will finally melt, the fire will fade, and knowledge will be victorious. I learned about these prophecies after the Operator, Evelyn, turned to me, after murdering her two nephews and told me, 'Immortality and divineness are curses. I wish not to live longer. You are Icy Heart and my rightful successor. End me and own your torch.'" She grabbed the gemstone from Proxy and approached me with it, and when I backed off, she handed it back to Proxy and moved closer again and tapped my forehead one time. "As seen, if I end myself without a valuable successor to claim and own the torch, all there is and all there was will no longer exist. Destiny led you here for a reason," she said.

When she finished, her snowflake iris melted a little. *She is not a monster by choice*, I thought and remembered all the times I had judged the Operator based on tales I had heard. *She's merely a being that experienced the burden that is immortality and the toll it takes on a soul. She wants out.*

"For them," I told her and asked for the gemstone. She pointed toward her heart. I obeyed and pushed the pointy end toward her heart. When the gemstone and her heart met, both she and Proxy melted before me, the way an ice cube does under too much heat. Like the famous third eye, a gemstone had carved itself on my forehead, but not until after my entire physical body transformed into a pure reflection of Evelyn. With all of this came all her memories. I, Alfonzo Ramos, had taken it upon myself to bear the heaviness that was immortality and divine to become the new Operator.

With my reign came the breaking of the cold and hot curse that was placed by the siblings of the Operator. Tri-Rail F made no more trips because I brought the glories of Destination One to not only the other destinations but all the way back to a place once called home, Earth.

28

Tales of the Operator

"Mr. Alfonzo, will you tell me the tales of this Operator?" Arian Jones asked, daughter of Bohen Jones who was brother of Lisa Jones. Arian pointed her finger directly at Evelyn Orionis amongst the four statues—Evelyn, Adamis, Adameous, and myself.

I looked at the statues and wondered if things would have ended the same if the tales of the operator that I knew were the same as the ones that the famous Operator knew. "You see, when Evelyn passed on the role of the Operator to me, I received all her family history, but deep in those memories, there is one that even the great Operator Evelyn never uncovered," I told Arian.

She looked into my red, snowflake-colored pupils (perk of being the Operator) with enough curiosity for every other kid who resided in Destination One and then begged, "Please, please tell me!"

"Go get the other young sea creatures. Let's make it an official story time," I replied. She obeyed. She ran on the grassy field, through the fruit garden, on the sand, and then dove into the ocean, changing her legs into tails, her thick red hair reflecting with the sun as she swam away. When she returned, she brought back eight of her friends. They all sat on the grass.

Before I told them the origin of the Operator, I had them all focus on Adameous Orinois, the one who began the story. He was the big secret in the tale, a secret that was so well hidden that even Evelyn never knew, a secret that was hidden so deep within the shadows of my mind that it was unlocked only when I became the Operator.

This tragic tale of the Operator began long before man existed. Though they had no idea how their existence came about, a trillion years ago, five beings found themselves on an ancient planet. This planet, though it is invisible to the naked eye of every existing being who inhabits our universe today, is located within the Orion Constellation, deep inside the star, Alnilam. These five beings were clueless at first. They wondered what they were for days until information ran through their brains like a computer that had just been powered. They had gained not only enough knowledge to name themselves accordingly, but also to unlock powers beyond imagination, powers which they used to begin a civilization on their own. These beings identified themselves as the First Orion, the Second, the Third, the Fourth, and lastly, the Fifth. One random day, the First caught a glimpse of the snowflake pupils of the Second for too long, and something happened, something so magical and new that it left the two of them paralyzed for almost two minutes. The Second's belly grew until the First looked away. Three days later, the Second had done something beyond any of their understanding; she gave birth. The other three stood with wide eyes and observed the miracle. The very first baby, a girl, was named Evelyn, and the second baby who looked exactly the same, except for her hair, was also a girl, was named Kiona. The two babies were almost exact replicas of their mother and their father, with skin as clear as snow and almost similar to Lemurian seed crystal, lips as blue as sapphires, one with long hair and the other with shorter hair.

The first girl, Evelyn, was given the name Knowledge, for knowing all was her signature ability among all her magical abilities. The second, Kiona, was given the name Nature. Her favorite part of it was ice, the primal state of their habitat. All could have ended there, but all the others backed up fearfully when the third child was born. The third child, Ibliss, who was given the name Deflect, had a unique look that was new to all the other Orion beings. With dark-brown hair, scarlet-red snowflakes for pupils, and a pale skin that often randomly changed into flame red, anyone, at any random time could've been affected by his deflecting powers, in one or more ways. Despite their differences though, all three babies shared something that the five Orion beings shared, a crystal at their forehead, a red tulip-shaped gemstone which they named a ruby.

When the triplets turned five years old, the Orions learned why each had been given one of those rubies. It had happened when the Fifth Orion stood close enough to Ibliss and realized how much he hated immortality. As if the information was hidden and then unlocked by the deflecting powers of the child, the Fifth knew exactly what he needed to do. As the others stood and watched, the Fifth Orion extracted the ruby from his forehead and plunged it in his icy heart. Like an ice cream sundae, the Fifth melted out of existence before their very eyes, and where he stood was something none of them had ever seen before. It was a book, the very first one.

The Fourth picked it up and found herself reading the words out loud, and all the others understood. The fundamental event forced all of them to beg for answers. The First removed the crystals from the foreheads of the triplets and hid them. He could not explain the feeling that pushed him to do this. For a reason he found strangely new, he could not let anything ever happen to them.

With Deflect's arrival, the entire planet had gotten affected, and by the time the triplets' fifteenth birthday came around, despite the First being the remaining of the first five, the planet had evolved. A new species, with the same architectural design, had populated the planet. The new species, which received many names throughout the years, came in different forms. Like baby ducks, at the first sight of the First, they quickly imprinted and became loyal to him and made him royalty, the first king.

When the triplets turned twenty years old, Deflect's powers had weighed in on the First; and he, too, had grown tired of immortality. The First sat them down and told them he was ready to go but not without passing on his kingdom. Without a debate, he called Evelyn forth and gave her the rights to his kingdom, the entire planet. Kiona stayed silent, but Ibliss could not help himself.

"But, Father, that's not fair. I would like to be king. You always like Evelyn more!" he said, and his pale skin began to heat up like a volcano preparing for eruption.

"Shut up, freak!" Evelyn told him.

"Well then," the First said, as he examined all three, "I will take a little vacation. When I come back for my final day, I will see who truly earns my kingdom. Whoever excels at the task more wins." He finished and then finally gave them back their rubies.

"What's the task, Father?" Kiona asked, with sudden interest.

"Kiona will lead my combatants. Evelyn will temporarily lead my kingdom." And after he finished, he looked at Ibliss and disappeared with him into a cave made entirely out of citrine crystals and ice. "This is now your own. Rule as you may, but limit how you deflect," he told Ibliss before he handed him a marble with dark blue-and-green spots.

"What is it, Father?" Ibliss asked.

"I call it Earth. It's a tiny play-size replica of our planet. I created little beings that resemble you so you can relate. To operate its insides, you'll have to connect with it through the magical force of your mind. You are their Operator." The First gave earth to Ibliss and vanished before Ibliss could object.

Thirty days later, on one snowy afternoon, as Ibliss spiritually, magically governed the little beings in his marble, his sister Kiona walked in the cave and observed. Inside the marble she observed something she thought was bizarre but new. "Those two beings are of the same sex. What are they doing?" she asked with burning curiosity.

"Yeah. I call it kissing. Usually it's a female and a male, but I think my deflect is affecting those two," Ibliss told her, and he did not seem bothered by it at all.

"And them?" she asked and pointed at a female and a male having sexual intercourse under an apple tree. Ibliss smiled and then said with a joyful tone, "That's Adam and Eve. They're trying to have a baby. They're having what's called sex."

Kiona turned her attention to another side of the marble and noticed something new, something that did not come with the marble. "That?" she asked.

Ibliss followed Kiona's gaze and explained, "I found a way to eliminate the ones that have deflected. The deflecting makes them do a lot of things father and Evelyn won't like, so I created that little station. It's like a correction station."

Kiona looked at the station and saw six little creatures with wings, at least to her they were little. Each carried hundreds of the little beings that Ibliss was tasked with governing. "I set them all with a random time. When the time is up, each one will be taken by one of those six dragons to one of those five destinations. Destination One is the ultimate reward for whichever ones are undeflectable by my existence. Only dragon one can take them there. Destination Two is when their deflects are severe to the point where it forces one to mess with the life or livelihood of another." Ibliss told Kiona, "Dragon number two takes them there, and when they decide to take responsibility for their actions and decide they will change, they can either find hidden ways out or dragon number five south or north will take them out of Destination Two and bring them back to Destination Five, which is Earth."

"What's the difference between dragon five south and north?" Kiona asked. She was certain Ibliss was not finished but just had to ask before the question jumped her mind.

"Well, dragon number five north takes them back as they were before time ran out right away, but with south, it may be years later, and their forms can change. They could end up as anything," Ibliss told Kiona, who had not realized yet that she was starting to admire Ibliss more than she should.

"What about those two?" Kiona asked and pointed two fingers simultaneously, one at Destination Three and the other at Destination Four.

"Destination Four is almost like two but less painful. It happens when one of them does not believe in magic, me, or anything. They'll suffer there for a little, and then one of the dragons named Five will take them back to Earth. As for Destination Three, it's just a bridge between one and two. Sometimes when one of them gets affected by me, it seems to make them happier, and so I feel bad to just send them to Destination Two, and so they choose their own fate at Destination Three," Ibliss finished.

Before his red lips could finally rest, Kiona's landed on them. He had deflected her finally. He had made her love him, something that was never heard of amongst the Orion population, something that only existed inside his marble of deflects.

Ibliss felt something awake inside him as well, and therefore instead of stopping the sickness that had fallen upon his sister Kiona, he pulled her in closely and exchanged some of his heat, warming some of her chills.

Days passed, and their newfound treasure, Love, had grown. As they operated together another afternoon, Kiona saw a pregnant Eve and became envious. "I want us to have babies, too, the way they do it. With you," Kiona told Ibliss.

Ibliss wondered if it was his deflect powers forcing her to want those things or if it was coming from what she felt for him.

"We can't. Father and Evelyn, along with everyone else, would hate us. It's not possible for us like it is for those beings," Ibliss argued as the two of them watched Eve eat an apple from a tree.

"If only there was a way for us to be in there. Be like them, even if it is for only a few hours every day," Kiona suggested, and though Ibliss knew the idea sounded crazy, it made him curious. At his first attempt at possessing a body inside the marble, Ibliss was successful. Immediately, Kiona followed him inside.

Ibliss jumped into the body of Lucian Ramos, part of his tenth class of creations, and Kiona jumped into the body of Ashandi Fazil, part of Ibliss's sixth class of creations. Every afternoon, Kiona and Ibliss meet at the cave and jump inside the marble together and forget about the life of divinity. Disappointment came down on Kiona after Ashandi did finally become pregnant but only within the limits of the marble. "What are we going to do?" she asked Ibliss, worried.

"I am as clueless as you," Ibliss replied as he examined the motionless bodies they had possessed, paused in place and waiting for another possession.

The two had not realized that Evelyn, who suspected something had been going on between the two of them, had gotten one of the combatants, by the name of Proxy, to spy on them. When Proxy reported the news of what Ibliss and Kiona had done back to Evelyn, the Orion kingdom divided in two, and war marched on. Most of the combatants, those that Kiona had passed the deflect virus to, remained loyal to her cause, but all of the rest stood behind Evelyn who vouched to put an end to the hybrid, unborn babies.

"They're unnatural, and Father will be furious if I don't rid you of them before his return!" she told Ibliss and Kiona before she promised them war.

Ibiza, a combatant loyal to Kiona, came to the cave one night with information on Evelyn and her side of the war. "She's heading this way," she told Ibliss and Kiona who stood over their marble, ready to suffer for their unborn twins. "But I managed to steal this from where she hid it. It's your unborn twins or her," Ibiza told Kiona and then handed her Evelyn's ruby of immortality.

At the sight of Evelyn's ruby, an idea came to Ibliss. "Our babies won't be born with rubies. She'll murder them to impress father, and there's no way we can win when she has three times the combatants we have, but without her ruby, she can't directly intervene with the marble," Ibliss said. Kiona and Ibiza listened carefully, as Ibliss added, "What if we use one of our rubies to keep her locked out of the marble forever by locking her ruby inside it."

"Something like that is probably not even possible. If it is, then one of your rubies won't be enough, and with your powers of deflect, the repercussions could be catastrophic. Don't do it," Ibiza advised.

"My love, it's better than the alternative!" Kiona said. At the beginning sounds of chaos outside the cave, she turned her fingers three times, and her ruby appeared like magic. "If something is to happen, I want you to go inside and defend my babies as best you can," Kiona said to Ibiza and transformed her less divine body into one like Ibliss and then sent herself inside the marble.

"The first you shall name Adameous and the second Adamis, if something happens," Ibiza heard from the sky after she became what eventually became known as a human being.

"I love you. Think of what you want most, and the ruby will obey once," Kiona reminded Ibliss who held three of the rubies.

After the last of their ice combatants had finally fallen, Ibliss kissed Kiona one last time before the crystals enacted. The powers of the rubies, mixed with Ibliss's deflect powers, had transformed Kiona into an ice blizzard that would take over a portion of the correction station, separating the two dragons numbered five, removing the exit routes from destinations that required them. The host parents of the twins, Lucian and Ashanti, had no recollection of the experiences but miraculously welcomed triplets instead, one of whom they never learned possessed the life force of Ibliss, along with all his memories, due to his deflect powers.

On the planet Orionis, Evelyn barged in with what remained of her combatants and found only a marble and another book. Evelyn saw something hidden deep within the crust of the marble—her ruby.

"I am doomed to live for eternity, Father," Evelyn cried in the arms of the First when he returned and learned of the war.

"My favorite," he began and then gave her the book and the marble, "you should know with every ruby used, there is a book for a reason. They used two rubies, and because their minds were linked to the same thing, there's one instead of two books, but worry not. If you fulfill the prophecies in this text, their curse will be reversed. You can finally rid us of two of their babies, make the third your successor, and then join me where I'll meet the Second and the rest," the first advised.

"How can I do that when I can't directly intervene?" Evelyn asked with desperation in her snowflake eyes.

"You have the gift of knowledge at your disposal. Manipulate it. Whisper into the winds of the marble and let the prophecies be heard by all, and let them fulfill them for you. There is not a thing their babies won't do to be reunited with their beloved parents if somehow they learn about them and believe there is a way to be reunited with them. Use your powers, my dearest Evelyn." When he finished, the First grabbed hold of his ruby and pressed it against his heart until he himself melted out of existence.

Evelyn took her father's final advice and did as he suggested, and with this, she became the famous Operator. However, despite having known all, having been Knowledge, Evelyn never knew that

Ibliss lived within Adameous and pulled all the right strings till the end.

* * * * *

"Wow, Mr. Ramos, does that mean Adameous was your first father, Adamis was your brother, and you were one of the triplets?" Arian asked after I finished the story.

"Yes. That's why I traveled the two fifth trains more than any being in existence."

THE END

About the Author

I doubt I'll ever forget RK Bates. It's impossible to forget the best person I ever formed a friendship with. My parents spent a lot of money to force me to move to Florida, to a halfway house. It felt like a curse at first, but the feeling changed completely after I met him. He went by King at that time.

After guiding me into a deep conversation after we met at Park Tavern bar in Delray Beach, during one of the nights I relapsed, King said to me, "I see people and the way they live life as a gigantic and scattered puzzle, some with more missing pieces than others," and I began to feel more sober. "I feel like there's particular individuals out there that can help them find their missing pieces, but I think it's a rare thing to even find those individuals. As that puzzle, being pieced together completely is still worth the effort though because I feel like that's the only task where the reward is unlimited happiness."

After that night, we agreed King would be my life coach and helped me through my recovery. In the end, everything he taught me, through word and action, did show me how right he was. After a successful recovery, I saw traces of King in my own behavior later in life. Always cheerful and sophisticated, I also became capable of being nonchalant and yet overly caring at the same time, highly intelligent, and through trials and tribulations, remained one of the strongest people I knew (mentally).

"I loved that guy. He was the best man I knew and still now he always crosses my mind. I would've made fewer stupid mistakes and suffered less had I met him a lot sooner," I often tell my husband and two boys. I said the same things to King when I saw him last.

Being the modest person he was when I knew him, he responded, "Maybe I'm just a creative mind cursed to live in alternative universes, doing my best to be a superhero to the few I'll have the chance to—the few who never had one."